Swansong

Swansong

A Message of Love and Farewell

presented and edited
by

BARRY HEAD

To order additional copies of this book, contact:
Xlibris Corporation
1-888-795-4274
www.Xlibris.com
Orders@Xlibris.com
38904

CONTENTS

PREFACE

From the Editor

I returned a while ago from Mexico, where I spend most of the year painting—mail not forwarded—to the usual carton of bills and catalogs. There will always be some Christmas cards that I open around Easter, and, if I'm lucky, a couple of actual *letters* from friends. This last time, there was a manila envelope in the pile of junk from an unfamiliar point of origin, addressed in a scrawly hand I didn't recognize. In it, I found a manuscript from an old friend of my parents. From what he says, he is over 90 now. I haven't seen him, or been in touch with him, since my childhood, and I'm old enough now to have a grandchild of 14. I didn't even know the writer had been my godfather until I read the letter he enclosed.

When I began reading the manuscript, I smiled. The tone was seductively warm and friendly, leading me on and on, and the contents came across as the fantasies of an amiable, but possibly deranged, old man. I found myself enjoying spending time with this otherworldly stranger with his unusual point of view. My feelings shifted, though, as I went on. His perspective on who we are and how we go about our business on this planet became unsettling and even, for me, a little scary. I don't think of the world the way he does, and I don't want to, but there was a lot of stuff he said that I couldn't argue with. Since reading what he wrote, my godfather's "love letter of farewell" haunts me. I can't get it out my mind. What if he *isn't* deranged? And if he isn't, do we have to conclude that we've really been living a monumental structure of delusions all this time?

At my age, I'm not about to change my view of things, but after thinking about it, it seemed to me that my godfather's farewell message deserved to be available for other people to stumble upon—and to make of what he wrote whatever they wanted. He'd said in his letter, as you'll see, that his manuscript was mine now, and that I could do anything I wanted to with it. All the same, when I finally decided to publish it, I thought I'd better check with him first.

Several parts of what he'd written seemed to me to need tidying up and clarifying, because, even after reading and re-reading, I'd lost the drift of what he was saying. He mostly went along with my suggestions, though he often sounded irritated at having to have anything more to do with what he'd sent me. In the case of some passages, he was adamant that nothing be changed, and they have me still scratching my head. Our back-and-forth was by telephone and email. As of this writing, we haven't been able to pull off a face-to-face visit, though we still hope to. He lives in a place that's hard to get to, doesn't travel, has recently had some worrisome, new, health problems, and in addition to all that, I'm in Mexico most of the time.

Here is the letter he enclosed with the manuscript. ("Beezer" is the nickname I remember him calling me when I was little. No idea why.)

> *Dear Beezer:*
>
> *This will come as a surprise, I'm sure. We haven't been in touch for so long! It was Dorothy Cartwright (do you remember your parents' old friend?) who somehow found me your address, and I hope it's your current one. Who knows these days when no one seems to stay put for more than a moment?*
>
> *I thought of you a lot while doing my rambling here. It was you I often imagined sitting in the old, overstuffed chair between the windows of the room where I sometimes write . . . but, I admit, more often snooze. I guess it's what people call a den, and that's really a pretty good name for it. I'm a very old badger now. You probably think I've been dead and gone for years. My next birthday, if I get to see it, will label me 92!*
>
> *I'm sending this to you, because I have no one else to send it to—and you were, after all, my godson. The rift that occurred between your father and me was stupid and unnecessary. While I'm sorry it happened, what I'm sorriest about is that it made me lose track of you. I would have liked to watch you grow up. Dorothy thinks you have children. I'd like to have had the chance to know them, too.*
>
> *Part of me said that it didn't matter if I sent these meanderings to anyone at all. That part of me, the part that has always made me an odd duck among you (no, alas, not a swan), was of course right. It didn't matter in a cosmic sense. But that more human part of me that I share with you asked me what good it was to write a kind of*

love letter if it didn't go to anyone. That's human logic for you! So I'm sending it to you.

I don't care what you do with it. It's yours now—yours to read (if you can get through it) or toss out, or whatever. If you want to share it with anyone, that's fine. The only thing I'd ask of you (more than ask: request, insist on) is that you leave me out of it. Entirely. Name, whereabouts, and all. This old badger is too old to be badgered by anyone anymore. What time I have left is my time, and I'm too stingy to share it.

Except with you, of course. If this were to spark a phone call, or even a visit, I'd like that a lot. (My number is 000-000-0000.) It would be a fair schlep for you to get here, I know, so please don't feel you have to. (Believe it or not, I do have e-mail. The address is xxxxx@xxxxxx. com and use it if you like.) If, before I exit, we get only as close as God and Adam on the Sistine Chapel ceiling, that would help put last things in order.

But that doesn't really matter, either.

I hope your life's been good to you and yours. Mine's certainly been good to me. As you humans would likely say, "Far better than I deserved." Puh-leeze! Who's to judge?

Affectionately across the years,
[his signature]

So, with his permission, I'm making my godfather's "Swansong" public. I can't tell you more about him, as should be clear from the instructions in his letter, but the truth is that I don't know much more than anyone else who reads what he wrote.

Barry Head

THE SILVER SWAN

The silver swan, who living had no note,
When death approached, unlocked her silent throat.
Leaning her head against the reedy shore,
Thus sang her first and last and sang no more:

"Farewell all joys, O Death come close mine eyes.
More geese than swans now live, more fools than wise."

(I remembered this from somewhere. I think it may be a familiar madrigal, but I don't know for sure and haven't any idea who wrote it. I may have gotten some of the words wrong, too, but I'm not going to bother looking them up. You can do that if you want to, because you have more time than I do. *Lots* more time, I hope.)

HELLO

Welcome to my cottage. Do please come in and make yourself comfortable. Take that old chair over there by the window. I should really have it re-covered one of these days, but I doubt I'll get around to doing it. Never mind. It's squashy and comfortable, just as it is, and has a way of embracing you. If I had it re-covered, I'm afraid it would look self-conscious in the midst of its long-time companions—the old, Persian carpet; the fading, striped, beige-and-yellow wallpaper; the dog-eared books; the leather recliner with split seams next to the fireplace; my scuffed-up, mahogany desk; and the "distressed" grandfather clock.

It's funny, that word "distressed." Interior decorators use it to describe something that's showing the ravages of age, and they even go to great pains to make brand new furnishings look that way. People, it seems, will pay more for that look, the way the young will pay more for "old" new jeans. Oops, sorry! I should have said interior *designers,* not decorators, shouldn't I? Like in the big cities, I'm told, a plumber prefers to be called a sanitary engineer. Well, I'm for everyone being called what they want to be called. If an actress wants to transgender herself into an actor, that's fine by me.

Where were we? Oh, yes, "distressed." *I'm* what's really distressed—in the designer's sense—around here. I have every right to be, for heaven's sake; I'm slipping into my tenth decade here among you. What you'd have seen through the screen door if you'd actually knocked (instead of opening a book cover) would have been a very old man with crows' feet and wrinkles and wattles, short in stature, and a good two inches shorter than once-upon-a-time, and white of hair but still plenty of it. Too much of it! It sprouts out my ears and nose as well. My friends tease me about my eyebrows. I'm sure you noticed them. They're like the bittersweet that grows everywhere around here, wild and tangled and out of control. My teeth are still good, I'm happy to say. My fingernails have yellowed, I have to say, and if I were you, I wouldn't look too closely at my toenails poking through my sandals. Of course now that I've said that, that's just what you'll do, and you'll see that they're like two families of tiny mud turtles plodding along with ridged and dappled shells.

Yes, I'm "distressed" all right in that sense, but far from distressed in the sense of upset or anxious. Absolutely not. Should I be? I have much younger friends who are already upset and anxious about growing old. But then they and I—and you along with them—have looked at life from vastly different vantage points all these years. It's the same landscape out there ahead of us, but the view we see isn't the same, and that has nothing to do with age, nothing at all.

But sit, please, do. Stay a while. I know, of course, that you're not really here. I'm not dotty, and I'm not writing fiction. Imaginary friends can be good friends, valuable friends, and that's what you are to me. You're even more than that; you're a *beloved* friend.

I know the lay of the land out there on the horizon. Wait! I wrote that too fast. I shouldn't have used the word "horizon" referring to Time and the future. At my age, the most distant "horizon" of that kind would be about an inch beyond my doorstep, and it would be the top of a steep and slippery slope. It's a slope that doesn't bottom out in a meadow of wildflowers, either. It's like a ski jump perched on the edge of the world. When I skim over that lip and soar, gravity's going to snap, and I'll keep on going, off into that wild, blue yonder, until I'm a tiny speck in the eye, and then only a memory, and then not even that. Bye bye. As I go, I'll hold my loving thoughts of you close to my chest, to my heart. I'll hug them as long as I can.

I'm luckier than you probably are, because I'm not afraid of the ski jump. I know I don't have to be. I so very much wish I could give you that knowledge along with this letter of love! Over the years, I've watched the fear of death cloud and constrict many a friend's ability to live fully and with joy. Please try not to let that happen to you. Life, for all of us, will stop when it stops. For me, it will stop soon, but until that split second, I will find joy in the changing light and shadow of the fields and hills beyond my window; in the sharp clash of ripe pears and blue cheese; in Bing Crosby and Satchmo swinging their way through "Now that's jazz!"; in the ambrosial smell of freesias; in the feel of slipping naked between the flannel sheets of a freshly-made bed on a chilly night.

That's a bit optimistic, perhaps. Depending how things go, my joys may not be so elaborate at the very end. They may come down to a sip of cool water, the press of a warm hand, and the sight of the kind eyes and comforting smile of a friend. But what joys those will bring me—right up until the light goes out!

Look around us now. The room is small, but the windows are large and open to one of late April's first balmy days. The painting between the windows is by an old friend. She finally broke away from orderly still lifes and landscapes and began smearing on textures and layers of colors with a palette knife. I'd always admired her representational technique, but when I saw this, one of her first abstract paintings, my admiration turned into absorption. I can look at it endlessly, even after all this time, losing myself in the depths of the ochres, gray purples, gray greens. What are the large shapes trying to tell me? Stability and peace? A pause before catastrophe? What's that flash of urgent orange shouting, there at the bottom left? The painting makes me ask questions and then reveals those questions as irrelevant. I like that. The questions are only in my head, not in the painting. The painting, titled "Untitled," is simply what it is.

You'll have to excuse the state of my desk—and I shouldn't even really call it a desk. It's a thick, mahogany plank on sawhorses, and though it must be about eight feet long, it's a rare moment when I can see the wood beneath the clutter. Books and magazines; printouts of to-be-answered e-mails; a marmalade jar holding blunt pencils; a postage scale whose cost indications are at least six postage hikes out of date; scattered audio tapes whose boxes I can't find; a fixed-wire telephone whose 5 is sticky and unreliable; cigarettes and an ashtray that's habitually full; and, for some reason known only to itself, a nine-inch Statue of Liberty wearing a proportionately small, straw, cowboy hat whose original toy owner long since bit the dust. Amidst this sea of confusion, my laptop rides the swells, a tidy, black raft which, in spite of its appearance, hides in its innards a confusion worse than that on my desk.

I look around and wonder why I can't keep things in order, why I can't throw more things away. I don't fret about it, though. Order will come when I'm gone. The room will be bare in no time. Someone will take stuffed, plastic bags to the dump, and that will be that. Shortly after, the whole house is sure to be knocked down, making room for something more in keeping with the current value of the land it sits on. Like me, the house will have had its time, served its purpose. It will be carted off as rubble, and I will be scattered as ashes. We'll be gone without a trace.

Some people, of course, leave footprints—by painting pictures and writing books, for example. Some of their works stick around for years, generations, centuries, even millennia. For those grandees as well, though, it only took a moment for their body warmth to evaporate from their passing footprints. Almost overnight, the heart that beat and mouth that spoke became only a name—an arrangement of letters carved in stone, or scrawled at the bottom of a canvas, or arranged tidily in black on a cold, white, page.

For instance, when the last person who actually knew the Emperor Nero died—the last person, that is, who could claim to have tugged on Nero's toga sleeve and (maybe) said, "Hey, old buddy, you got a light?"—when that last person was gone, Nero Claudius Caesar became the title of a story, a legend, a myth, as larger-than-life, and as lifeless, as a Macy's-parade mega-balloon.

I'm not trying to leave footprints here as I write. For starters, I'm not a writer. All I'm trying to do is give you a farewell gift, along with a hug. My life here among you has been, as some of you would say, "a trip." I've lost count long ago of how many times I've gotten high on human life, how many times its strange chemistry has blown my mind. As a trip in the sense of a voyage, my life has taken me through many an awe-inspiring landscape, but travel is risky business. I've suffered my share of detours and derailments, shipwrecks and emergency landings. Who hasn't? It's the way things work here, no matter which travel agents you use along the way to plan your life's journey.

But I don't want my money back. Certainly not! Despite the glitches, I got my money's worth if only for one reason: I have loved and been loved. I have fallen deeply in love, and stayed deeply in love, with my human companions like you. Yes, even with you, O nameless, faceless shadow who assaulted me that night on the streets of Pernambuco. My wounds healed. I know that what little you got from me did nothing to heal yours. Face-to-face with any of you, I'm like one of those out-of-control, head-in-the-clouds, star-struck lovers you so often write about, compose songs about, make movies about, and I'm not ashamed to admit it. What can I say? I may be what I am, but a big part of me is as human as you are.

Ah-ha. Is there some mystery here? Do we need X-Files music fading up in the background? No and yes. No, there's no mystery, and yes, you'll go and make it one, no matter what I say. You're made to play detective, to go sleuthing out even uncommitted crimes. It's as irresistible a compulsion for humans as hopping in bed with another warm body—a delicious moment that has often made me grateful for my strictly human side.

When I tell you about myself, I'll look blurry to you, out of focus. The X-Files, if I remember right, has a tag line that goes: "The truth is out there somewhere," the *somewhere* being out there in space. That's getting warm.

What makes me different from you is that what's "out there" for you is "in here" for me. You're made of the stuff of this planet. I'm made of that, too, but I'm soaked in the great cosmic brew out there as well. It infuses every cell in my body, making my thoughts and feelings and perceptions different from the ones you have. That cosmic stuff softens my edges. I don't end abruptly at my skin the way you do.

Whoever came up with the phrase "the music of the spheres" came up with a lulu. It's poetic, and poetry, like music, has a way of softening the hard edges of the human mind. It dampens the paper on which the ink of human sensation is spilled. It makes the harsh, black strokes run, makes them bleed seamlessly through gray back into white. When you talk about "losing yourself" in something, the way I can lose myself in that painting on the wall between the windows, you could say that something dampened your paper, that the sharp division between what's outside the skin and what's inside it grew fuzzy for a while. Some people get "lost" in activity, some in stillness. That's how I feel all the time.

Those soft, lost moments feel good, don't they? They feel sort of like you're unclenching a fist. Measured minutes, even hours, collapse into a timeless place without beginnings or endings. That's when you're closest to "the truth that's out there somewhere." But your paper dries quickly after such a dampening. Your mind sets up in hard edges again. Not so for me. My paper stays moist all the time. Compared to you, yes, I'm a blurry creature.

I see you frowning. Have I lost you already? Stay with me, and try not to complicate the simplicity of it all. Trust those blurry feelings you have from time to time, because that's when you and I come closest together. Let your edges get soft. It's the key to your being able to accept this legacy I so desperately want to leave you as I skim off the ski jump's lip. Lean back in that comfy chair now and just listen. Turn off the analysis switch. Pretend, if you like, that all I'm doing is telling you a story.

I can't begin with "Once upon a time," though; that's the whole point. This story would have to begin something like, "Ever and for always" instead. "Out there," as you put it, there are no beginnings and endings, regardless of what the books say. There's a lot of "stuff" up there in what you call the sky, and it's doing a whole lot of dancing around. The music of the spheres that accompanies the dance never began and will never stop. I don't know any word for that ongoing event, and I doubt there can be one. The very idea of "never" or "forever" goes against human understandings, goes against the way humans are constructed and are able to understand anything.

What is it that runs through me? What is that stuff out there? This isn't a matter of Science, which is lucky, because Science was my worst subject in school, closely followed by Math. All I know about Science—and this I do know because of my otherness—is that Science won't ever be able to understand, let alone explain, what's going on out there. It can do away with various kinds of superstitions, that's for sure. More than that, it can make your world, as you see it, ever more logical, predictable, measurable, and pliable. Science can go on mapping, more and more precisely, the insides of the "house" of human perception, but it can never break through its walls.

Knowledge is a wonderment, and gaining more of it is a joy you'll have as long as there's one of you left to go on asking "Why?" Your passionate pursuit of knowledge is one of the characteristics I love and admire most about you. I like knowing, too, that you'll never run out of new things to learn. Scientists already accept that to open one door is to reveal new rooms, rooms with new doors, but few, if any, accept that that's how it will always be. Scientists, after all, are only human, too, and so they still chase after the beginnings and endings of things.

For instance, there may have been a Big Bang, for all I know, but if there was, it wasn't the first, and it won't be the last. If Science finds to its satisfaction that such an event did indeed take place, it will be because things have been Big Banging all along. So where did "everything" come from? It didn't come from anywhere. It's always been everywhere. When did it begin? It never began and will have no end. Like I said, beginnings and endings "out there" have no meaning. There's only change, always and forever. I know it seems to you that everything has a beginning and an end—a story, a song, a symphony, a journey, a vacation, a horse race, day and night, the year 2000, love, and, of course, even your life itself. Here on Earth, as processed by that odd knob that sprouts from our necks, beginnings and endings mean a lot. But out there? If there were any consciousness out there to think about anything, the notion of beginnings and endings would seem like the bizarre, aberrational imaginings of a truly off-the-wall species.

I'm going to end up complaining a lot about language as we go along. It's such an inadequate instrument! Sometimes, however, accidentally, words approach the barrier of the inexpressible, which is where you and I are standing now. There's a phrase that's still having its moment in the sun as I write, and it's "Go with the flow." It's caught on, I think, not only because it's short, simple and catchy, but because it casts the shadow of something we can't quite get our hands on, can't even name. I like phrases like that, but, alas, they tend to have a short lifespan. I suspect sometimes that they get put to death on purpose. Having words running around that evoke something unnamable, something that can't be counted or measured, can be scary and threatening, particularly to those whose business it is to name and count and measure things.

Come to think of it, it's not only simple, obvious phrases that suffer bad fates. Simple, obvious music, like those yearning melodies of Tchaikovsky and Rachmaninoff that so easily touch me, have been banished to the Siberia of the "popular" and "trite." Simple and obvious paintings, such as representations of sunsets and sad-eyed children that get straight to the point, get labeled as "motel art" and considered by the intellectual set unworthy of so much as a glance. To get back to simple and obvious words expressing simple and obvious things, if I were to quote *The Prophet* these days, I'd be considered corny as well as old and soft-headed. "Go with the flow" won't last long. The sophisticates among us have already stigmatized it as belonging to an airy-fairy, New Age reincarnation of old hippydom. I can see them wrinkling up their noses at the whiff of marijuana that clings to its edges.

But that's all a detour, forgive me, and I hope you will, because my mind tends to ramble around a good deal now. For better or worse, I've gotten to like the way it wanders, and we're sure to do a lot of detouring together so long as you have the patience to stay over there in that chair. Back to the point: Whatever people think of "Go with the flow" these days, I'm going to go with "The Flow"—capital T and capital F—as a way to talk with you about what's happening out there, or up there, or whichever "there" you prefer. Simple as it is, it's not easy to talk about, but it only gets harder trying to intellectualize it. You may be an intellectual, for all I know, but not this old dog. So let's do something simple and obvious and look out the window.

Over there on the right, just beyond that first, low rise in the field, you'll see a pond. From here, you can't see the hammock I've strung between two of the trees on the left of the pond, but it's there, and it's a favorite place of mine to take naps. On a warm afternoon late last October, I woke from one to find four deer drinking not 20 yards from me. I must have been downwind, or perhaps my scent of senility had reassured them that I wasn't up to doing them any damage. I stayed still, and when they were done drinking, the deer ambled off as if they hadn't a care in the world. Geese sometimes land on the pond and stay awhile between appointments. I particularly like the iridescent dragonflies, which skim about and even get bold enough to land on my hand and stare me in the eye. The way they copulate on the wing the way they do, flitting and darting all the while, leaves me full of admiration. Copulation used to be hard enough to pull off in a hammock! I've seen small fish of some kind jumping about on the surface of the pond, frogs jumping in and out of it, turtles snoozing in its water up to their eyeballs, but I have no idea what all is going on down in the depths.

Whatever it is that's going on down there, it certainly isn't mindful of me in my hammock. It's The Flow flowing. And if it flows down there at the bottom of the pond without so much as a thought about you and me, why should it flow any differently up there above our heads?

Maybe there's something about water that can make it easier for us to talk about The Flow. Maybe it's not a coincidence that "go with The Flow" suggests water. After all, they say this planet is mostly water, that we're all mostly water ourselves, and that whatever it was that became human came crawling out of water once upon a time. I have all that second-hand, of course, but that's what the people who look for the beginnings of things have to say about it.

Here's what I've picked up along the way about how water seems to work on this planet: It rises from the oceans, and it pours down on the mountains, runs through the valleys, and seeps into the earth, forming huge underground puddles. I can see that everything water touches is changed by its touch, and it must be that everything touched by water in some way changes the water itself. I've seen a clear river cloud up as it meets a tributary that has run through different country, and the land upstream must have shifted and eroded under the water's passing. Water in wells and faucets is different all over the world. It's different even from neighborhood to neighborhood. "Designer" waters in pretty, plastic bottles are different from one another. It's all water, though.

I'll take it on faith that we're mostly water. We drink it and let it out, changing it as we send it back to where it came from. Everything we eat seems to depend on water moving through the plants and animals. Sinking my teeth into a medium-rare filet mignon, just as surely as my emptying my bladderful of beer, has to be a way of letting water move through me as it makes its way, back to other waters, changing the natures of those waters as it rejoins them. The single bead of sweat that evaporates from the top of my head will, I suppose, eventually change in some way the nature of all the water on the planet.

Imagine, then, that "The Flow" I'm talking about is something like the "water" of the universe. It's not wet, of course; it's more like what humans know as vibrations. It's everywhere, moving through everything, rising in different shapes here and there, dissipating again, altering as it goes, on and on, forever and ever. And then goes on for as many more "evers" as you have the patience to add.

Human beings are forms The Flow just happened to take, as are all the forms of things you know or can imagine—even "imagination" itself. The Flow doesn't take forms on purpose, any more than The Flow of water here on Earth takes forms or does anything on purpose. The Flow has no purpose. "Purpose" is only a human concept, a way for humans to talk about certain kinds of behavior they see around them. It's a mistake, I'm sorry to say, to take a purely human concept like "purpose" and look for it anywhere else. "Awareness" is another of those concepts. The Flow is not "aware" by any definition that humans have given that word. You know what awareness means, but it only has meaning to you and among yourselves as you try to describe different life forms on your planet.

This is hard going, isn't it? It certainly is for me, because language wasn't made to describe things beyond human experience. Let's come at it from a slightly different direction.

From your point of view, something has to be *something*, right? One trouble about talking about The Flow, even giving it a name, is that it isn't anything particular, and giving it a name suggests that it is. If it's anything I can approximate in words, it's a flow of Possibilities. In it are all the Possibilities of everything you can think up—and then so many more Possibilities that you *can't* think up that the idea of numbering them has no place anymore. People talk about infinity and an infinite number of things, but I'm not sure "an infinite number" makes any more sense than "one hand clapping."

It's hard, I know, to think of a place where neither numbers nor counting things works. Here, we'd be in bad shape without numbers. But numbers are sort of like a bucket—useful in some situations and meaningless in others. A bucket is great for scooping water out of a boat or catching a leak, but what use is it for scooping sadness out of the heart, or catching a cold?

A second difficult notion to understand is that when a Possibility occurs, takes shape, bursts forth—like human beings, for instance—that Possibility may be more like the nature of The Flow itself, or it may be less like it. For example, any Possibility that pops up might have an endless amount of Possibilities within it . . . or it might not. You humans don't. From your perspective, it may seem like you have a vast range of Possibilities, but that's only in comparison with other life forms you know. I don't mean to sound rude—not now or ever, believe me—but in terms of what's possible "out there," well, you're handicapped. You're both cursed and blessed not to know it.

Here's where I come in. The Possibility that became the human species resulted in billions of different variations on the theme, and, if you're careful, will result in billions more. As we all know, no two variations have ever been, or will be, identical. It can happen that one of those variations ends up with blurred edges, like I have, where the boundary line between The Flow and a particular Possibility that took shape out of it is faint or isn't even there at all. That can happen, because that, too, is a Possibility.

Look out there at the pond again. Imagine the difference in nature—in taste and smell and life and what goes on—between that pond and a tidal pool. Water moves through them both, but water of a different kind, and it moves differently and with different results. There may be times when the pond and the pool look very much alike, as you and I in many ways look alike, but The Flow moves through me in a more tidal way than it does through you. It makes me different, yes, but in no way special in the sense of superior, or having strange powers. What I do have that you don't have is a closeness to The Flow and, because of my humanness, a constant *awareness* of that closeness.

I've often wished that I didn't have that awareness, because it sets me apart from you. There are many things that happen in a pond that can't happen in a tidal pool, and of course it works the other way 'round as well.

I don't know about you, but I've done enough difficult thinking for the moment. If you find what I'm saying hard to understand, pity me for my struggle to find ways to say it! I'll do something easier now. I'll share with you a little of what it's been like to live as I am.

One of the things that I haven't been able to do is father children. I've always had plenty of juice, but 0 sperm count. That may be just coincidence, but I'm inclined to believe it's a result of my "otherness," the way what lives in fresh water dies in salt and vice versa. Apart from that, my body functions sexually the same as the body of any healthy male. I married twice. My first wife—long, long ago—left me to find the life she wanted and the children I could never give her. We stayed friends as we both readjusted to being single again.

That there were no hard feelings when we split was generous on her part and natural on mine. I don't feel feelings with the same intensity you do. I know sadness and anger, jealousy, the longing for revenge, the satisfaction in an enemy's downfall, but those feelings, *all* my human feelings, are somewhat distant, objects of curiosity and interest to me. They come and go as they will, but leave a large part of me, that part that is of The Flow, untouched. Among you all, this separation of feelings from self appears as a lack of feelings, rather than a different way to understand feelings. I didn't realize what this would mean in a marriage. Even the fact of marriage itself didn't involve me totally, the way you seem to think it should involve the whole person. Looking around, I'm not sure it ever does, but that's purely for reasons of human nature. In my case, it never could.

From my first wife's perspective, this distance that I had from my feelings made me hard to live with. She was a budding psychologist, and she thought that I'd been shortchanged somehow in childhood. Even though I was an only child, she thought I'd never had the chance to "bond." Little did she know, and still less could I explain to her, what was going on. After a time, our lives went in different directions, and we lost touch. I know she married again and had children. I hope she lives happily ever after.

I married again, too. I had learned a lot the first time around. I felt I had a better understanding of your expectations of human marriage, and I believed that now I could meet them. The one expectation I could never meet, as I've said, was fathering children, so I was careful to choose, and be chosen by, a woman who didn't want any. Some of the people who knew Monica considered her "spiritual." Others thought she was "other worldly." To still others, she was simply a "kook." We were both in our early 40s when we met, and our slow-growing mutual attraction got stronger as we gradually came to appreciate that neither of us belonged in the usual, everyday world. I had to spend a lot of time there to make a living. Luckily, I was more willing and able to play the games of that everyday world than she was—and much better at it.

Monica and I had our differences. She was an activist, and I wasn't. She didn't carry banners or march in parades, but she spoke out. It disappointed her that I didn't. She spoke quietly, but ardently and intelligently, about human rights and animal rights, about the waning health of the planet. She upset people with her unshakable convictions and made them nervous by so openly living them out in her own life. She was a total vegetarian, wouldn't wear animal products, hated synthetic materials, sheltered a menagerie of woebegone creatures, meditated, and periodically went on terrifying fasts that I was sure would kill her.

She was not a "joiner." Clubs and organizations of any kind, including congregations or any formal gatherings with an odor of hierarchy, turned her off completely. Much to her credit, she tolerated my not living by any strict principles and my belonging to a number of organizations that seemed necessary because of the work I did and the people I knew. Most of the friends I grew up with, and a highly privileged bunch we all were, remained warm to me after my second marriage, but chilly to us as a couple. I think they thought it was too bad that I'd gone and married such a "drag."

But they didn't know the Monica who smoked pot—organic, of course— drank moonshine liquors—home-made—and, when the conditions were just right, danced naked in the dewy grass of the short-cropped meadow beside the house. Most of those dances took place in early spring or early fall, at first light of day. The air would be still, the rising dawn would shimmer on the wet meadow as on a mirror. Monica would stand for a moment, poised on the lowest of the porch steps, an alabaster statue. Then, to some inner music which I could almost intuit, she would set off like a figure skater into the meadow. Dots and swirls, arcs and even circles, would emerge beneath her, all strung in a sequence that left the meadow a perfect record of her ecstasy. Done, spent and breathless, she'd fling herself into the blanket I'd be holding ready for her on the porch. The blanket would grow warm in my arms and then gradually cool as the sun broke the horizon and we watched her meadow art evaporate into the sky.

On a very few occasions, the circumstances were just right for Monica to dance under a full moon. Once, she tried to carve a word for me into the glistening, white marble of the meadow. When she was done, we hurried to an upstairs window for a clearer view. I thought I could make out an "a," a "p," perhaps an "l," but the word remained a mystery, and Monica wouldn't tell me what it was. She led me, smiling, to bed, and we lost ourselves in one another, me lost in her as much as I ever could be lost in anyone. As she was falling asleep, she stroked my cheek and said, "That was the word."

Our skeptical friends didn't know the Monica who adored sex, and that was fine by me—both that she adored it and that they didn't know.

My otherness kicks in now when I say Monica was a fascinating human study, and that she certainly was. My humanness, though, overtakes me in the tears that still well up when I tell you about her—if only this little bit—and have to get to the point in the story where she was killed by a freak electrical storm in the Colorado mountains.

There's part of me that's just as human as you are.

If there have been down sides to being what I am, there have been up sides as well. One, for instance, is that people have always thought I was "a nice guy." I've made friends easily all my life, moved comfortably through foreign cultures and different levels of society. I've been singled out repeatedly as a safe place to deposit confidences. I can take credit for some of it—the part of it that I figured out, learned, and then carefully put to use.

For instance, I made myself a good listener, but that wasn't hard because I'm so interested in how you 100-per-cent humans think and feel and act. It's easy, too, to listen to people you love. I'm hesitant, reluctant even, to give advice, because I've learned it's more than likely to be wrong. I'm comfortable trying to help people sort out decisions for themselves, usually just by listening well and letting them talk. When they make decisions that turn out badly, at least those decisions are their own.

I don't talk a lot, but that came easily, too, because I don't feel I have much of substance to say that anyone can understand. I can chit-chat in a friendly fashion along with the rest, but when a conversation takes a serious turn, I find myself out there in my own left field. What's more, it seems to me my human mind is sluggish. When it comes to voicing an opinion on the spot, I often can't, because I need time to think.

Not talking a lot made it easier for me to keep secrets. It was harder for me to learn not to make promises I couldn't keep. For years I found my affections and good intentions tripping me up and letting people down. I don't know why it should have taken me so long to realize that you can't break a promise if you don't make one in the first place.

All these are ploys—obvious ones, really. They lead to odd outcomes, though. Listening well has made people think my conversation is interesting. Not giving advice has made people think I'm clear-headed about their dilemmas. My silences have made some people think I'm wise. Not making promises has made people think I'm trustworthy. Sometimes I feel like a charlatan.

What I can take no credit for, of course, is being, by accident, what I am. That accident, more than any of my ploys, has made moving among you easier for me than for most. I've traveled widely in your world and lived for long periods of time in different countries on four of the seven continents. I enjoyed encountering new customs and behaviors, adapting myself to new versions of "good manners," and immersing myself in the philosophies of new belief systems. For me, it was like moving through a wondrous botanical garden where all around me sprouted varicolored flowerings of the human imagination. Whereas cultural differences from one another often set you at odds with one another, your differences were my delight. My sadness was—and is—that you so seldom truly rejoice in each other's multi-hued colorations.

"What do you mean?!" you say. "My wife and I just paid an outrageous amount of money for tickets to go see the Ukrainian Folk Ballet. We *loved* it! What's more, next summer we're going with a group to Thailand and Viet Nam. That'll be *really* colorful!"

You bet it will! And Macchu Pichu and the Taj Majal and the Acropolis, along with the cultures from which they rose, are marvels for sure. They're monuments to human ingenuity, human ability to give thoughts and ideas form and substance, and the universal, unstoppable, human urge to find expression for what you variously see as "beauty."

Is it Ubangi women who put ring after ring around their necks until their necks are as long as their forearms? "Oh, honey! What do you mean you forgot to bring the camera?"

I'm not making fun of anybody here. I'm merely commenting on the obvious: Enjoying human diversity as a spectacle is different than rejoicing in your daughter's inter-racial marriage. If I could only find a way to let you feel your microscopic, insignificant, brief and inconsequential place in The Flow, the superficial differences that divide you would seem so trivial compared to the unlikelihood of your existence in the first place. From that vertiginous—but accurate!—perspective, you would find yourselves clinging to one another to keep your balance, finding comfort and reassurance in the kinship of your species.

In all my travels through different cultures, I've seen young children everywhere who craved to play with water, chased after pigeons, wanted to be comforted as night falls, and who needed to be reassured that people they love, who have gone away, will come back again. Is there such a thing as a culture without lullabies? And in all the vastness of the cosmos, only humans sing them.

I gave up traveling a while back when the fun went out of it. I liked it better when it took longer to get places, when there was time to watch the changes along the way. Now it's grit your teeth and get there fast, see as much as you can, and then grit your teeth and get home. I'm old-fashioned, I know. Of course I'm old-fashioned; I'm *old*, for heaven's sake. I flew on the Concorde once. I didn't like moving faster than sound. I'm so old-fashioned I *like* hearing the sound of things, dammit!

But even if travel itself had remained fun, I'd have stopped. Little by little, the joy I'd once found in different cultures waned. I came to feel I was hearing the same sad music again and again, only orchestrated differently. It was like a cantata that opened with a hopeful children's chorus, modulated to romantic madrigals, swelled to battle hymn, and ended with widows and orphans singing a requiem for the dead.

No matter how it seems to you, you all are so *alike*!

You frown, and I don't wonder. I am speaking in generalities and don't seem to be taking into consideration, for instance, the multitudes who, over time, have preached non-violence, refused to bear arms, and suffered for their pacifism. I seem to overlook the helpers of this world who, in different times and in different places since the beginning of history, have risked, and often lost, their lives as they courageously tried to alleviate all kinds of human suffering.

I do take them into account and feel humble before them. But where even the warmongers and the peacemakers, the breakers and the menders, tend to be alike is in their doing their thing in the name of a higher cause or concept—because, for instance, it's someone's idea of the *right* thing to do, or because, perhaps, it's someone's notion of a Manifest Destiny of some kind.

What I know because of my otherness is that there is no higher cause or concept that is not a human invention. All your remarkable constructions of philosophy, religion, and metaphysics have been crafted to deny what is unacceptable to you—that is, the impersonal neutrality of The Flow and your appearance within it *by accident*. There is no Grand Meaning to your life. Grand Meanings are illusion and wishful thinking. Because that's what they are, they are vulnerable and need to be heavily guarded against any gusts from the winds of doubt. That's why ploughshares get beaten into swords and pruning hooks into spears. Life simply unfolds in its own way for each of you, as it has for me. We get to make a lot of choices along the way. The outcomes of those choices present new possibilities, and on and on we go until our particular light bulb goes out even as new ones are lighting up around us.

It's all so simple: *There is*, and *you are*.

"There is"—forever, and oblivious to you. "There is" an eternal flow of change going on about you. It has no human attributes, no human awareness, no human feelings, and no human form. You can neither identify it nor quantify it. It never began and will never end.

"You are"—for a short while, and of meaning only to yourselves. "You are" part of The Flow, one outcome of its infinite possibilities. As a species, humans, alone, have human awareness, human feelings and human form. As an individual, your particular form does have a beginning and an end. Humans have a remarkable capacity to identify and quantify, but only such things as a human brain is able to encompass . . . and that does *not* include The Flow.

That's all there is to it.

Yes, that's the big picture. But slipping into the small hotel room of the human skull, and flinging open the twin windows of the eyes, and stepping out onto the balcony of the human senses, you see a marvelous, miraculous landscape. It's a landscape you long to explore, because it's yours, and there has never been, and won't ever be, another like it. It feels like home to you, because within that landscape you *can* have meaning—there, and *only* there.

Perhaps that's why I fell in love with you. For coming on ten decades, I've had meaning to you, and you, for sure, have had meaning to me. "Out there" beyond ourselves, we have no meaning to anything. That makes us pretty special to one another, doesn't it?

You look skeptical and, yes, a bit sleepy over there in that chair. No wonder. I'm not making myself clear, I know, but I don't know how to do better. To make matters worse, I'm being unclear about bad news you don't want to hear in the first place. Take a break. Go outside and get some air. You'll see a path just to the right of the door that will take you through a pine grove. In the middle of the grove there's an open space and a very comfortable stump to sit on. You can't miss it.

But come back, please. Come back, and we'll muse—lightheartedly, I promise—about what we're stuck with here: those unreliable, deceptive, slippery and slithery things called "words."

CAN WE TALK?

The older I've been getting, the harder I've been finding it to get messages through to other people the way I want them to be heard. I don't think it's senility, but that's a possibility, of course, because if senility is the culprit, I'd be the last person to know what's going on. What I find myself doing more and more is stopping short of saying what I want to say, because I know it's going to be heard differently than I meant it, so why bother? So I'm saying less and less these days, and it's lucky I can't get much older or I'd be walking around, mute and looking stupid, with everyone saying, "Poor old fellow, his mind's gone."

Something's coming back to me, something, from Gilbert & Sullivan. (I had a G&S "phase" back in college.) If I remember right, it's part of a song about crime and punishment, and a pool shark is sentenced to spend the rest of his days in a dungeon.

> And there he plays extravagant matches
> With fitless finger stalls,
> On a cloth untrue, and a twisted cue,
> And elliptical billiard balls.

Or something like that. Anyway, that's how I feel trying to send a message from my brain to my mouth through someone's ear and into the corner pocket of his or her brain. I'm definitely behind the eight ball.

Trying to "talk" to you through words, printed impersonally on a page, only makes things worse. I don't know if there's anything to the business of analyzing people's character through their handwriting, but if you were reading this love letter in my very own longhand, complete with crossings out and flourishes, I think you'd get some sense of my personality that you can't get here. It would be better still if you really were sitting over there in that armchair by the window where I'm imagining you. Then, at least, we'd have the loudness and softness of our voices, facial expressions and body language to clarify our intentions and shade our meanings. We might have a better chance of getting our messages through to one another—better, but still, it seems to me, not very good.

Many years ago, I was traveling through west Texas with a Latin American friend of mine, Gustavo. We were driven off the road by a torrential rainstorm and took shelter in a roadside bar to wait out the storm. Gustavo's English was somewhere between poor and dreadful, but he did his best to make conversation with a burly, likkered-up guy on the next barstool who wanted to know where Gustavo was from and where he was going and all those sorts of things. I was getting the same treatment from the fellow next to me, who, as I remember, seemed to think the Northeast of these United States should be hacked off the continent and set adrift. Even I found myself treading the line carefully between friendly banter and fighting words.

I could hear out of my left ear that Gustavo's conversation had moved on to politics and farm subsidies and cattle prices. The only politics Gustavo knew anything about were the politics of graft and corruption, and as for the rest, he didn't know any more about subsidies and cattle than he knew about quotas and taxes on yo-yos in Singapore. The Texan, I could hear, was getting riled up about something. Maybe Gustavo's abundant body language was coming across as evasive and dismissive. Whatever it was, he was obviously in over his head, and he decided to go get his English phrase book from the car. Getting up off his barstool, he made the gesture from his culture for "I'll be back in a minute"—his thumb and forefinger half an inch apart—and turned to leave.

Well! The Texan grabbed Gustavo by his shirttails and yanked him around face to face. "Fuckin' wetback!" he hollered. "My dick's big enough to rip you a new asshole!"

Come to think of it, we use tons of gestures so naturally that we don't even know we're making them, don't we? There are all those little movements of the eyebrows, the shoulders, the arms, legs and feet. How about those we can't control even if we want to, like changes in breathing, and the dilations and contractions of the pupil of the eye that I've read about? I hate to think what unintentional messages I've sent in the foreign languages and cultures I've floundered about in.

Here's a puzzle for you: How come, after all these thousands of years of increasingly congested cohabitation on this planet, you humans haven't come up with a shared language? Why hasn't that ever seemed the obvious, desirable and simple thing to do?

I know how come and why, and I know it because of what I am—and because of what I'd so much like to give you, which is distance from yourselves as a species and closeness to The Flow. Like I said before, if you could only see yourselves from "out there," you'd feel a deep kinship to one another that would have made you, long ago, crave a shared language in addition to the beautiful varieties you grow up with. But that's not the way it is, I know, and it makes me sad for you. What you have to live with, instead, is the all-too-human need to dominate one another. That built-in need, it seems to me, follows closely behind your needs for food and shelter, and it's not always a bad thing. Again and again, your need to dominate has been responsible for sudden, astonishing leaps forward in all aspects of your lives. As far as bringing you all together, though, forget it. It's only served to unite small groups, estranged from one another and often hostile to one another, as they pursue their different beliefs and purposes.

I can imagine a time when humans could only communicate with one another by grunts and gestures, but even then, the sounds of the mouth and the wavings of the hands that were accepted in one valley would have differed from those in the next valley. Even back then, it wasn't in human nature to get together on shared snorts and snarls—far from it! Human nature is such that the folks in Valley A insisted that the folks in Valley B do it their way—and vice versa.

I can see a standoff on the mountain ridge dividing the valleys. There, defiant, stand two hairy creatures, each backed up by a gang of glowering, fellow-valley Neanderthals, the womenfolk, their babes in their arms, shifting about uneasily on the edges. The rival gruntings get louder and louder, the body language more and more aggressive and menacing. We don't need an interpreter to understand what's being said.

"Our grunts are better than your grunts!"

"The hell you say!"

"Your grunts sound like a saber-tooth puking!"

"You call your things grunts? Wooly mammoth farts!"

And with that, one group beats the other to death. The survivors, swaggering a little unsteadily, herd the new supply of women back to the ranch for a good time.

There was no one who could say, "Hey, just a minute, guys! They've got a neat kinda snort for 'drizzle' we could use. How about we sit down together, grunt it over, and see what we've both got to offer?" No one came up with that option, because back then, human nature didn't offer such an option. Such a thought didn't even exist to be thought.

"Wrong!" some anthropologist is shouting from the back row. "There are tribes of happy, primitive natives where it's aggression that's the unknown concept." Maybe so. In The Flow of infinite Possibilities, that's a Possibility as well. But I'll bet my bottom dollar that there's a swanky resort now where those happy natives used to frolic in the surf. Or soon will be.

Who cares? Certainly not The Flow, where there's no "who." That's how things work here, and only you can care—if you want to. You and I both better face it: Without the drive to dominate, you wouldn't be flushing toilets before getting to work on wheels. You wouldn't be flying through the air to visit The Pyramids or Angkor Wat. You wouldn't be flying *anywhere*, and those attractions wouldn't exist. Nor Venice, nor the chateaux along the Loire, and, most certainly, not the Tower of London. We can add to that the Sistine Chapel, all the music of Haydn, the Beatles' *Abbey road*, Diego Rivera's murals, and Oprah Winfrey's book club.

One day, there probably will be a common language for you all. If you ask me, it will be a language that already exists. It may get modified a little on the way to its domination of the others, but it's not likely to be an entirely new one someone has thought up. The huge disinterest in Esperanto makes me think I'm likely to be right. Someone asked me the other day what language was spoken by the most people on Earth. I made the usual guesses, but I was wrong. "Bad English" was the answer, and it's probably the right one. In the language stakes, English does seem to be leaving the pack behind. All I can say is that, poor linguist that I am, I'm certainly glad I didn't have to learn it from a book.

Even when it comes to supposedly good English, as spoken by native speakers across the United States, we can have a tricky time communicating over the simplest things. When you increase the size of the arena to include English English as well, a fag is not a fag anymore, and poking someone doesn't mean in the eye. See what happens when you go still further afield to any of the far corners of the globe where English was left as a legacy! A legacy of what? Why, of domination, of course.

But let's stay closer to home. Let's stay in the city or town where you live. Can the blue collars and the white collars talk to each other with any accuracy? Up to a point, I suppose. For instance, imagine this telephone conversation:

"You mean you want me to come out at this time of night on friggin' Christmas Eve to fix the waste trap under your kitchen sink?"

"Yes, that's exactly what I mean."

Or: this face-to-face conversation that took place later on:

"You mean 15 minutes' work just cost me 300 bucks?"

"You got it, buddy."

What the words don't say, not even with facial expressions and body language, is that with 14 people staying in The Big House for a family reunion to celebrate the first Christmas without Grandpa, the kitchen sink meant something special. Or that on the other side of the tracks, getting out of warm bed and a hot girlfriend was a real pain in the ass, particularly as that blissful, interrupted moment was likely to have been all that was good about Christmas, given that the wife had just up and left with the kids, the split-level was about to go into foreclosure, and the pickup needed a new transmission.

I read somewhere about how we bring our own "inner dramas" to everything we see and hear, and you could add to that everything we smell and taste and feel, as well. When it comes to words, I can understand that all but the innocent little articles and particles and such can be charged with unsaid meaning—even if the voltage is low and doesn't shock us. Every single word carries its own electricity, unique to its generator.

Just take the word "electricity" itself. To a family that doesn't have any, it may be a dream. When the rates go up for a senior citizen on a fixed income, it may be a hardship. To an inmate on death row, it may be a lot worse than that.

How did I get to this word "electricity," anyway? Was it an accident, or was my subconscious at work? To me, it means a phone call, lightning in Colorado mountains. It means a tragedy and a sadness from which not even my distance from human feelings could insulate me at the time—and still can't.

I don't want to talk about electricity anymore. In fact, please excuse me, but I don't want to talk about anything more right now. I'm going to make Rascal, who in dog years is way older even than I am, take me for a walk. Stay where you are, please. I won't be long.

*   *   *

I feel better now. The daffodils are up along the driveway, and who could not feel better for daffodils?

A major reason that I want to leave you this mash note is that you spend so much of your time here hurting. I know that pain, too, and I know that when it comes, nothing, not even daffodils, can make it go away. The only thing I've ever found that eases it is the word of a loved one, even though any loved one can tell you that trying to bring comfort in words is like trying to carry water in a sieve. A hug is better than words, the holding of a hand. Those, alas, I can't give you.

Small and inadequate as I may claim words are, they're mighty, irresistible tyrants as well. It seems to me they begin bamboozling us when we're defenseless babes, conning us into accepting their domination by offering us the most effortless of sounds—the "ma-ma-ma" that rewarded us with comfort, smiles of approval, and warm milk. Before we were old enough to suspect that something was afoot here, those sounds took the form of Mama, herself—that huge presence who organized our lives and told us what was allowed in our new world, and, more to the point, what was *not*.

Keep in mind, of course, that this is just the way I see it and not some pronouncement of someone who knows anything about this business. And here's how it seems to me the unequal game on that unlevel playing field continues:

Inside our cocoon of human potential, independence starts struggling to get out. When it chews its way through the walls, it doesn't look anything like a butterfly—not unless you know a species of butterfly with machine guns mounted under its wings. Our rebellion against Big Mama is a pitifully one-sided affair, but, to keep the game in play, those tyrants, words, slip us a little ammunition. "Ma-ma" shades easily into "na-na," and one day on the battlefield, we find ourselves with a smart bomb: "No!" It was an easy weapon for us to get hold of, because Big Mama was leaving it lying around all the time.

Then comes learning the names of things. Most of us don't remember our caregivers endlessly pointing to body parts, pictures in books, and at things around the house, coaxing us into repeating their names. If you've had children, however, you'll certainly remember doing it to your kids. It's a game that's played all over the world. Though we may not be able to remember playing that game in our infancy, you can bet there's a part of us that remembers the rewards that came with our getting the answers right: claps and smiles and hugs. The punishment for getting things wrong, of course, was frowns and scowls. I'll bet it seemed to us like if we got something wrong, those big people wouldn't love us anymore.

You bet we learned! And as fast as possible! Those things over there are called "spoons." It didn't matter that there are thousands of kinds of spoons in the world. At first any old spoon was a spoon. Then came adjectives, letting us sort out the differences in spoon land, letting us get the particular one we wanted. We thought we were acquiring mastery, but, if you ask me, we were sinking deeper into word slavery. By the time we could speak in complete sentences, our bondage was tight and secure.

What no one told us—not because they were mean-spirited, but because they didn't realize it either—was that each new word we learned came with a pair of saddlebags. In one of the bags were all the meanings and conventions our culture and the people around us, put on, say, "spoon"—things like what spoons were to be used for and how they were to be handled. We were sternly told, for instance, that they weren't meant for banging on the tray of the highchair or for throwing on the floor. In the other saddlebag were the feelings we, personally and uniquely, through our individual experiences, had come to associate with "spoon." Early on, it might have been the unpleasantly aggressive way this object got forced into our mouths, sometimes with foul-tasting yuk, or, on the contrary, the comforting feeling of its breast-like shape on our tongues. (Later, a spoon might signify, more than anything else, time for a fix and a high.)

I think of the way we learned words and their commonly accepted meanings as a sort of a freshman course, Culture 101. The chances are we finished that introductory course around the age of four or five and moved on. Now, it wasn't only our first caregivers who were shaping our world with their words, but a whole bunch of other people around us who were putting in their two cents as well. The most influential of this cast of new characters were, I suppose, our first school teachers. They insisted—it was their job to insist!—we learn and adapt to the concepts and conventions of our culture. Part of the reason for our being sent to school, after all, was to get us "socialized." The explanations and negotiations that trying to socialize us required obviously relied heavily on words. My intuition tells me that the way words get strung together in any particular language has a lot to do with the way its speakers come to think about abstract concepts, but, hey, I'm not going *there,* thank you very much!

Where I think I'm going with this free-for-all speculation, though I'm never sure where my mind will end up these days, is that big notions end up in small words—words that not only carry the distinct coloration of a shared culture, but, on top of that, shades of that color that are unique to each of us because of our unique experiences with the concept that word is meant to represent.

If I use "fairness" with you in a conversation, for example, assuming that you and I got socialized in the same culture, we're likely to act as if we both know what that word means and get on with our discussion. If we were to dig deep though, excavate beneath the surface shorthand of the word "fairness," I'll bet we'd uncover some surprising differences between us as to how we feel about that particular combination of eight squiggles on the page, or the two-syllable noise they make when spoken aloud. If that's true between you and me, children of the same culture, how can we expect the concept of fairness to be understood by our cousins in, say, Saudi Arabia? And let us not forget this: Each of our cousins over there will feel somewhat differently, because of his or her unique experiences, about whatever their nearest equivalent to our word "fairness" may be.

It's a wonder we get along as well as we do, even if it's not very well.

In the end, our whole world comes to exist within the confines of words, to the point where everyone behaves as if something that can't be named with words either can't matter, or can't even exist. Well, maybe not *everyone*. There are always some people who look for a meaning to life in precisely the unknowable and unnamable, the ineffable and the numinous. But that's defying the tyranny of words, and that defiance is treason in most cultures, and treason is something for which you can be put to death.

So, can we talk? Can we understand one another? Within our shared culture, only vaguely and imprecisely, and across cultures, only distantly, indistinctly and confusedly. Even talking to you, I feel I'm trying to cross an abyss on a mere thread strung through a row of greasy ball bearings. In my bare feet. Far down below, I think I hear the snarls of ravenous crocodiles. I've had to resort to such an extravagant picture, because I don't know a word that describes the obstacle that prevents my being able to tell you how different The Flow is from your human understanding of your world. I can't even describe The Flow itself, because there are no words for it, either. "The Flow" is just another picture idea, one that may, at best, give you some kind of *feeling*.

I'm not about to give up, though. Love doesn't give up easily, does it? Maybe a little bit of what I'm trying to tell you will get through. People call me a lot on cell phones these days, and often their voices are all broken up and crackly. All the same, I can usually make out a word or two, enough to get the gist of what they're trying to communicate.

Can you ever break out of this bondage of words, language and culture that restricts so tightly the way you see your world? I don't think so. If you could, you'd no longer be human. *If.* An English friend of mine, long since departed, used to get outraged at the hypothetical "ifs" that people dropped so frequently. "If, if, if!" he would bellow at the offender. "If my aunt had balls, she'd be my uncle!"

Some people grow up in more than one culture and may speak, read and write more than one language with the fluency of a native. Yes, their perception of their world will be different from that of a one-culture person like me; but, no, they won't have broken free of a world defined by words. They will have more of them to use than I do, and they will be able to string them together into more concepts than the rest of us have. What they will have gone and done, in fact, is bind themselves up in even *more* bonds than we have.

I haven't ever heard of a culture built on the notion that there is only an eternal flow to things, a flow without beginning or end, without caring, design or purpose, a flow that encompasses everything and in which nothing "matters"—as humans use that word. Odd individuals may, from time to time, and here and there, have claimed that such is the way of things, but so far as I know, never a culture. Those individuals were, indeed, considered odd, and generally they came to bad ends. If they were lucky, they were simply ignored. If they weren't so fortunate, then they were most likely rejected; and if not rejected, locked up; and if not locked up, summarily offed. I'm one of the lucky ones, because I was born into a culture where the worst that could have happened to me was to be ignored or rejected. So far, I haven't suffered even those outcomes. That's because, up 'til now, I've been careful about what I say and haven't let any of those fickle critters, words, betray me.

It's not that I've been a coward. What I'm telling isn't a cause that needs someone to raise a banner, a crusade that needs an army. I'm not out to prove anything or change anyone's mind. You are, by nature, what you are, and even if I wanted to change you, I couldn't. You'll go on being loving and lovable, as well as hard on one another and yourselves, as long as there are enough humans left to inflict wounds . . . and other humans to bind them up. I don't want to change you. All I want to do is leave you a gift that could make your life so much easier if you were able to accept it. This message is nothing but a token of affection, and you're free, of course, to trade it in for a size that fits you better, or even swap for something you'd rather have. If only it didn't have to be wrapped in words! *If.*

Speaking of which, I'm getting tired of wrapping so many words in quotation marks, and you must be tired of receiving them that way. But what am I to do? Quotation marks are the only way I know to signal that even the best word I can come up with is nothing more than a poor approximation of what I want to say, of what I *feel*. I'm afraid we're going to be stuck with a lot of those damned quotation marks. When you see them coming at you, let them remind you, please, what inadequate tools we have to work with.

It's a shame we can't do better talking to one another. It really doesn't seem fair, does it?

It's Not Fair!

When you look around at what's going on in the world, there's so much that doesn't seem fair, isn't there? There's hunger amidst abundance, poverty amidst wealth, plagues amidst well-being, repression amidst freedom, and on and on and on. There are many things you and I may disagree about, but on this I'll bet we don't: Some people get the goodies, and others, frankly, get screwed.

It's been my experience that psychiatrists are a rum bunch. I look back at the ones I've met, and more often than not they've been contradictory characters. They lead disorderly private lives, even as they spend their time trying to put other people's private lives in order. There's one psychiatrist I value a lot as a friend, and he's no exception. His own life is a jumble of ongoing alarms and confusions, but he has a waiting line of patients who are desperate to see him, because, it seems, he's very successful at what he does professionally. I can see why he would be. At times, socially, when someone gets talking about a knotty emotional situation, he inadvertently dons his psychiatrist's hat. His whole demeanor changes. It's almost as if, for a moment, he becomes someone else. You can see his listening mode kick in, and after he's thoughtfully and carefully listened for a while, he'll quietly come up with some penetrating insight that none of the rest of us could have thought of.

On one occasion, after he'd come up with one of his zingers, someone said, "Wow! I can see why your patients love you. You're so damned rational about people's problems." He laughed, and said, "No, not always," and then went on to tell us how, a few days before, he'd gone and "lost it" with a patient. His patient was a man who was in the toils of loss, divorce, failures at work, and who knows what else. He was feeling hard done by, feeling that life had done him dirt. "And it's not fair!" the man complained.

My friend the psychiatrist said it was that whining complaint that made him lose it. He slammed his hand down on his desk and shouted, "Who the hell ever said life was meant to be fair?"

It may have been unprofessional behavior on his part, but, all the same, it was another of his penetrating insights. Of course life isn't meant to be fair. Life isn't meant to be anything beyond energy that accumulates, bounces around for a while like those ping-pong balls in the lottery machine, and then disperses again. Only you can invent a meaning for life. The ways you all try to do so is a big reason why I love you.

Concepts like Liberty and Justice are grand inventions. They're such uniquely human concepts, ideas that are as much a part of being who you are as heart, and lungs, and, of course, that convoluted wonderment behind your eyes that looks like stony coral but is softer than eggplant. If only it were not encased by the curvature of the skull! If only it were housed in a bowl instead, open to the full extravaganza of the skies! If it were, you'd marvel at how much the brain looks like coral, rather than at how much coral looks like the brain.

You're frowning. Was that a "Huh?" I heard?

That last sentence wasn't just fluff in the wind. There's an important thought there, embedded in my eggplant. I was out the other day with a friend of mine, Anna, and her six-year-old daughter. Someone said to Anna, "Amazing! You look so much like your daughter!" Anna replied, "I think it's the other way 'round."

Am I splitting hairs? Maybe, but it's a way to suggest how natural it is for humans to consider themselves greater than All Creation. Regarding All Creation as something lesser than humans, it's understandable to wonder at the surface similarity of coral to the brain. But a little humility, please. Coral's been around a long, long time. Humans are late comers to the scene and likely to depart it well before coral does—at least if we can halt its destruction by human hands. Coral looks like the brain? As my friend Anna said, "I think it's the other way 'round."

Back to Fairness. Imagine the tomes and tomes and tomes that humans have written about liberty and justice. If all the world's written material that bears on liberty and justice were gathered together, entered into a computer in 12-point type (about the size of these letters you're reading), and transferred onto a computer's hard drive, why I'll bet it would fill at least half a dozen of those things. And I'm including everything that has to do with law and legal systems the world over—even the contents of those red, black and beige volumes that seem to be in every lawyer's office and regularly turn up in the background behind television "experts" when the producers want to make the experts look credible. I've never noticed what turns up behind those experts the producers *don't* think are credible, but have to be given air time because of the media's "fairness" doctrine. Now there's a research project for someone! Might that background turn out to be shelves and shelves of MAD Magazine?

I'm being facetious, I know, but perhaps not altogether. There's nothing trivial or ridiculous about the relationship between foreground and background, and the effect the one has on the other in this world of yours.

Don't take me seriously, either, about my speculations on how much has been written about liberty and justice—not that I think there's any danger you will. I have absolutely no idea how much of anything fits on a so-called hard drive, nor even how it's measured. In different kinds of "bytes," no? Gigas? Megas? I once held in my hand a trilobite. It was a rock-solid, clam-like thing. I hadn't yet had my 20th birthday. The trilobite, they told me, had had its four millionth and then some. One hard-drive "measurement for dummies" that's used hereabouts these days is how many times one of them could hold the contents of the Library of Congress. I admit to being a real dummy, because that doesn't help me at all. Maybe all the tomes that have been written about liberty and justice, the paper and print ones you can hold in your hand, could, if they were cemented together, build a building the size of the Library of Congress. Maybe three and a half Libraries of Congress. Even with good cement, though, it wouldn't hold up as well as the trilobite.

It occurs to me that however much of this liberty-and-justice literature there may be, all but a tiny little bit of it almost certainly has to have been written in the last 300 years. I feel confident saying that, because if you go back more than 300 years, there wasn't a lot of either liberty or justice, as we now like to think of them, floating around to write about. What makes my assertion even more secure is that even if there had been a *lot* of liberty and justice about, there weren't a lot of people writing about anything at all. Not a lot of people, by today's standards, even knew *how* to write.

Three hundred years! That's only back to the time of my great great grandparents. How densely packed human events have become in that short time! How obsessively centered those events have been on liberty and justice! But what's been in the foreground and what in the background? Have all these events taken place up front, downstage, against the hazy backdrop of those two lofty ideals? Or have Liberty and Justice been out front, the one, with bared breast, striding forward waving a flag, the other doing her best to keep up with her sister, despite her blindfold and awkward balance scale, while in the background, upstage, massive armies swarm to and fro across the scene, the colors of their uniforms blurring into an indistinct, dappled-dark-red mosaic?

I see my high-school English teacher poised with red pencil over that last sentence, but to hell with it; I'm old enough now to write what I want, and, besides, she not only didn't last as long as the trilobite, she didn't even last as long as I have.

Whichever way you choose to see the foreground and background, liberty and justice are newcomers on the block—as the headsman observed, honing his axe. Before they stuck out their necks, life was simpler. Emperors and kings and popes and mullahs and shahs and maharajas and various tribal leaders with unpronounceable titles decided who had the freedom to do what and how justice was to be served. The model seems to have been the family: Dad knows best, makes the rules, and does the spanking. It was neat and tidy—until Mom and the kids dared speak up. "*My* turn to play dad," said Mom, and, chimed in the kids, "We get to make our own rules for a change!" Of course they were bound to speak up! They're human beings, too.

"Indeed!" said the enlightened Founding Fathers. "That's what this is all about, this is why we're wearing out so many quill pens writing tomes and tomes. Go for it! In fact, it's such a fine idea, my beloved sons, that you get to go out there and die for it young. But remember: No voting until you're a grownup. My beloved *white* boys, that is. The rest of you unfortunate males will have to wait. And you, honey, well, you and the girls will have to wait right along with them. Trust me; Dad knows best."

Oh my. That makes me think about my father. He was a loving man, but given to excess in everything. I wish you really were over there in that chair and could tell me about yours. Did you grow up thinking your father's decrees were always fair? I doubt it. I doubt anyone does. I certainly didn't. No matter what age we are, we're in a different time and place than our parents. Our *context* is different than theirs, and because it's different, we have a different concept of fairness.

There ought to be a word for taking an idea, an idea that is both necessary and practical, and making it so big it doesn't function anymore. A parachute can be a practical necessity, but if it was so big I couldn't get out the airplane door when I needed to, I'd want to complain to the management. A little salt in a recipe may be a good thing, but only a lunatic cook would conclude "the more the better." That reminds me of a phrase I came across somewhere: "To over-egg the pudding." Its quaint ring makes me think it must be English. Perhaps "getting carried away" with something is as close as words will let us come to the idea I'm in danger of getting carried away with here, the notion that "enough is enough, but too much is just right."

The egg of liberty and the salt of justice may have their place in combining the ingredients of a society into a tasty pudding, but as any cook should know, proportions do make a difference. Is it really a good idea for Liberty to be dashing across the battlefield waving aloft a banner emblazoned with "MORE EGGS & SALT!"? And would somebody, please, help that poor lady behind by taking off her blindfold and letting her see where she's going?

Speaking as a human, I don't know how much freedom I really want, or, for that matter, how much I want *you* to have. I'm much more comfortable out there on the road—yes, I'm still driving at my age—knowing you haven't got the freedom to wheel around full of high-octane liquor, and that if you think you do, you won't be at liberty for long. As for me, well, when that E at the top of the eye chart wriggles like a snake that doesn't know if it's an F or a B, they'll take my license away. Being human, I'm going to feel ambivalent about that. I want my freedom to drive, but I don't want to end up killing any of you, whom I love.

There was a time when, even without glasses, I could read the second line from the bottom of that eye chart. Did I ever want my freedom then! I was working in a big city, handcuffed by the watch on my wrist, confined by bus schedules, ordered around by deadlines, and shackled to the ball and chain of insufficient funds. My inner human burst forth like Spartacus, and overthrowing the tyranny of other people's expectations, I loaded up a backpack and made my way to a palm-frond shelter on a remote beach in a far-distant country—a country that the human yen for freedom has led to changing its name twice since I was there. I did take my watch; busses, boats and trains had schedules. But the further I went, the less useful my watch became. The numbers on those schedules grew more and more approximate, until they might as well have been ants, wandering across the leaflets with no sense of direction. Conveyances came and went, or didn't. They went in the general direction I was heading, or they went somewhere else. I eventually got to my beach, and there, under my shelter, with a hammock, my backpack, the sea and me, I was a free man. I awoke that first morning of the rest of my life to a crimson sun, turning red and then yellow as it broached the water and took to the sky. Naked, I walked out into the warm ocean to greet it, as though reversing the whole sequence of evolution. When the salty broth of creation was lapping at my bellybutton, I took off my watch and hurled it as far out beyond me as I could.

Now *that* was liberty! It lasted about as long as my watch took to fly from my hand and sink, with hardly a splash, beneath the swells. I turned my back on the sun, dove beneath the surface, crawled onto the beach, pulled myself erect, and strode back to my shelter like the first human on earth—which, clearly, I wasn't. My backpack was gone.

I've taken to using "liberty" and "freedom" interchangeably here, and I wouldn't want you to think I was being careless with words. Like I've said, we have so few of them that we ought to do our best to use each for its intended purpose. A screwdriver can open a beer can, but if there's a "church key" around, it will do a better job, and while that kind of church key *might* get you into a church, I wouldn't count on it.

I feel a nuance of difference between liberty and freedom, as you probably do, too, but it's not easy to pin down. Liberty seems grander. It's "freedom" gussied up a bit so that it won't look out of place in good company, like the company of Equality and Fraternity, and, yes, Justice. When you're moving with *that* crowd, you'd better be properly dressed, and liberty looks better than freedom wearing the white-tie-and-tails of a capital letter. (Even sailors, at liberty, are expected to look well turned out.) Liberty's bell sounds with a more stentorian tone than freedom's ring. It has a louder voice, even in the human throat. "Give me liberty or give me death!" made it into the books. "Free me or kill me" wouldn't have stood a chance.

To me, freedom feels more comfortable with shirtsleeves rolled up, getting on with the job. Freedom is more at home struggling to get out of jail in bare feet than striding through the Halls of Justice in shiny shoes. Countries get liberated, slaves get freed.

For all that, I find the two words are often hard to distinguish from one another, especially in their every-day clothes of lower-case first letters. If either of them turns up capitalized here—except at the beginning of a sentence, of course—you'll know I'm nudging you in the ribs, asking you to think Big. Otherwise, I'm going to go on using them interchangeably. I'm going to feel free to do that; I'm going to take that liberty.

How did I get out of my predicament on the beach? I sat for a time beneath my shelter, sucking the bitter gumdrop of my sweet freedom, and then I walked, stark naked, of course, and under an already broiling sun, to the little village a couple of miles inland. I caused quite a stir when I appeared, bright red in back and white, white, white in front, as strikingly bi-colored as the Swiss flag—not that my coloration was what made the men dash out of their huts and the women flee into them, while the naked children sucked their thumbs and stared, wondering what all the fuss was about.

Adults in that community, for all I know, may have enjoyed a lot of freedom, but they weren't free to expose themselves as I was doing. The men gathered around me, frowning and scolding and shaking their heads. With gestures, I tried to convey that I had nothing to wear, which they were slow to believe; they'd seen me come through the village the day before, decently clad, with backpack and all. With the utmost disapproval, they thrust some cloth at me, made it clear I should cover up, and then pointed back down the path to the beach. I squatted stubbornly, and using the first two fingers of each hand, acted out the theft—me going for a swim with my right hand, and, with my left, someone sneaking up, grabbing my backpack, and running off with it. Who needs words, anyway?

Then the real commotion began. Disapproval turned into outrage. The men held a swift conference, came to clear agreement about something, and headed off like a posse. In no time at all, they returned, frog-marching a male adolescent and holding aloft my backpack. Apologies are apologies in any language, or no language at all. The head honcho made it clear I was to keep the cloth they thrust upon me as a kind of peace offering, or, perhaps, award of damages. As for the unfortunate adolescent, he was ordered to hang onto a post and received, then and there, a sound thrashing—no hearing, no plea, no prosecution, no defense, no verdict, no appeal, and no lawyers' fees involved. Dad spanks, Mom wrings her hands, and that's that. Justice prevails.

Thinking back on that incident, I see liberty and justice—with their sleeves rolled up—at work. But what if that unfortunate adolescent had protested that he wasn't the one who stole my backpack, that it was his no-good cousin who took it, and, unbeknownst to him, hid it in his hut where it was found? And the cousin denied the accusation? I suppose there would have been a hearing of some kind, where each cousin got to tell his side of the story, and then the village leader would have sorted it out as best he could, Solomon-style, in all his wisdom.

Does justice look any better than that, even when it dresses up as Justice? I don't think it does, and it may even look worse. Stains and patches are more unbecoming to fancy clothes than to jeans and a tee shirt. Marking out the boundaries of liberty and justice is manual labor in the fields, not a court quadrille. I think the dress-up part is no more than the need to camouflage the limits of human possibility—namely the complete and absolute *im*possibility for you humans to attain ideals you've set up as Ideals when those Ideals run counter to the very human natures that set them up in the first place. All the court finery that goes with the quadrille—the silk and lace and powder and perfume—camouflages bodies that often haven't had a proper bath in weeks. I've heard it said Versailles in its heyday was a stinky place.

How much freedom can a person stand? Is it really a heresy to answer, "Not much"? I know that out there on my isolated beach, even after I recovered my backpack, I soon found myself inventing things to do, to occupy my time. At first the need to eat took up a good deal of that time, for which I was grateful, but then the villagers took to leaving nightly care packages for me under the sea grapes at the top of the beach. I began making up projects and schedules—at what regular times (by the sun) I would swim, eat, explore, whittle, nap, swim, eat, jot in my journal. I needed my freedom to be tempered by structure. My mind began a persistent campaign to come up with a reason to walk to the village, to borrow the *village* structure, and though I never did, that part of my mind never gave up trying to win me over. My human nature craved human companionship. But I'd set up the Ideals of Freedom and Solitude; I would stick by them to the end.

My human nature won, as it was bound to. Despite the difference in perspective I have from the rest of you, knowing that whatever I choose to do doesn't matter in any real sense, I am here as a human being and with all that brings with it. When my human nature realized that I would stay intellectually steadfast in pursuit of my Ideals of Freedom and Solitude, it simply flowed around the barricade I'd set up and flooded the landscape nonetheless: I would, I comfortably decided, preserve my Freedom and Solitude so long as I stayed at the beach . . . but I wouldn't stay there as long as I'd planned. I walked back out after only a little more than two weeks, nature and intellect back together where they belonged, and both happily satisfied.

That's not quite right, though that's how it felt. My nature and my intellect weren't ever really apart, and so it makes no sense to talk about them reuniting, any more than it makes sense to talk in separate terms about the mind and the body. To set up unattainable ideals, and then fail at reaching them, *was* my nature, just as it's yours. You and I, think what we will, are imprisoned by the government *of* our nature, *for* our nature and *by* our nature. We're imprisoned there, because we are the jailers as well as the inmates. We can't stage a successful jailbreak against ourselves. Even if we could, we'd find there's nowhere to break out *to*. The difference between you and me is that your nature makes you go on inventing imaginary landscapes beyond the prison walls. That much, at least, I've been spared. I know there's nowhere to go except back to the infinity of the stars.

What could have been more natural—of my human nature, that is—than to have craved, there alone on the beach, the companionship of the villagers? If I'd given in, my ideal Freedom would have had its capital letter knocked off in a jiffy. When two or more are gathered together in thy name, O Liberty, the sparks will fly. If we don't want the whole barn to go up in flames, we'd better call in your sister, Justice, and have her standing by with her fire brigade. Its engines may be held together with chewing gum and baling wire, its ladders full of busted rungs, and its hoses ruptured at the seams, snaking back to a water supply as illusory as a mirage oasis on the desert horizon. But never mind all that; the firefighters have nifty uniforms.

You and I know that, in groups, we can't function by doing whatever we want whenever we want to do it. We beg to have that freedom taken away from us, or, more accurately, to have that freedom taken away from everybody else. Take traffic lights, for instance. They're not there to keep me from running into other people. They're to keep other people from running into *me.* Let us be free to holler for Freedom, give us the right to clamor for Liberty, but please, oh please, don't take us at our word!

So how much liberty do you suppose is enough? The answer may be: just the basics—enough to keep most of us quiet, focused on things other than revolt, and not a jot more. And what are those basics? How free do you want to be? My guess is that you'd find as many answers to that question as the number of people you asked, because the word "freedom" has no meaning without a context—you know, freedom to do *something*, or freedom from *something*. All by itself, it's just a little helium balloon blowing about in a bright, blue sky. The problem is that each of our lives is led in a different context, a context of its very own, unique unto itself, and so freedom's little balloon looks different, depending on whose wrist it's attached to.

Fine. But this carnival's not going to be any fun if we run it on a zillion different answers. We can't have everyone clambering onto the merry-go-'round at once, or let people go wandering around among the bumper cars. We must have order, we need a standard. The good news is that we have one. The bad news is that we seem to be stuck with it. Here in this country, we have the Constitution and The Bill of Rights.

If you or I were a modern-day CEO of a global corporation, would we want our company run by 18th century rules and regulations? I wouldn't. Oh yes, the Constitution is meant to be amenable to amendment, but it's about as easy to "mend" as it is to keep on patching a pair of worn-out socks with one hand tied behind your back. And The Bill of Rights? There's not one bit of it that doesn't need a "but" at the end—like the "but no yelling *Fire!* in a crowded theater" bit. The Constitution and The Bill for Rights got things off to a promising start, but so did the quill pens they were written with. We have computers now. Just as Freedom takes on different meanings in the different contexts of individual lives, so does it inevitably alter, it seems to me, as times change the contexts of social groups.

Here's human nature doing its thing and getting carried away again. (And yes, I know, my human side is getting carried away with this whole subject, but it feels good, I'm having a good time, and I'm not stopping.) The ideals of the Constitution and The Bill of Rights were already unattainable back when they written, and they are even more so today. They were written for a species of a different nature than yours, an idealized species. To cover up the reality gap, they were given capital letters, which, like the Red Cross on vehicles in battle, meant no one was supposed to shoot at them. They have been given their place among The Sacred Cows.

And isn't that a sweet little shepherd boy back there in the cloud of dust, herding the Sacred Cows along, or are my eyes deceiving me? Bless my soul, they *are* deceiving me! Why, it's that naughty old Emperor on the loose again, wandering around in his birthday suit! Somebody should tell him he's not allowed to do that! As far as I know, it's not in The Bill of Rights!

To me, Liberty looks different from the way she's usually portrayed. I see her as a young woman, with as yet no fulsome breasts to be bared, no flag held aloft above the carnage of battle. She's wearing a demure summer dress, a sunbonnet on her head, and she's carrying a bouquet of wildflowers across a meadow. She's far too young for me—at my age, who isn't?—but there's no doubt that her innocence is seductive; it makes you want to hug her tight. It makes you want to kiss her rosebud lips. But be careful, she's a handful. She grew up in a dysfunctional family and never got properly socialized. If you kiss her, watch her eyes carefully. Behind those fresh lips she has fangs.

Her older sister is supposed to be keeping an eye on her, and sure enough, Justice is there in my fantasy wildflower meadow, too. She left her blindfold and scales back at the ranch, but even so, she's having trouble keeping up with her little sister, who's tripping on merrily ahead. Justice looks rather spinsterish as she strides through the goldenrod, hoiking up her long skirt with one hand and trying to hold her parasol *and* shoo away the summer flies with the other. She reminds me of a stern, humorless governess, Mary Poppins without the magic, and like Mary Poppins—forgive me Julie Andrews, my angel—way short on sex appeal. Poor thing! She's doing her best at what must be a thankless job.

Justice may be austere, and of the two sisters not the one who catches our eye, but I think it's Justice, more than Liberty, we should be courting. When we get together, we fight, and more important than whatever it is we're fighting over, sweet Liberty included, is bringing our fisticuffs to an end before someone whips out a stiletto—and uses it. To me, at least, that's the famous "bottom line," though it beats me why Priority Number One should end up at the bottom, even if it's only at the bottom of a metaphor.

Justice has not yet found a way to prevail on this planet, at least not the kind of justice you've crowned with a capital J. It won't ever do so. It *can't* ever do so. A sow's ear can no more turn into a silk purse than lead into gold. It's not in the nature, the essence of the things, and those "things" include you. You cannot transform your essential nature into the nature of imaginary angels, but what *is* "angelic" about you is your refusal to believe you can't fly, no matter how many times you fall off the roof. One of these days, a whole lot of you seem firmly to believe, you *will* sprout wings.

A dreary admonition, from somewhere in my past, is shouting to be heard. All right! All right already! BUT . . . keep your voice down. Freedom of speech doesn't include busting my old ear drums. So, all right, lay the admonition on me.

"Wise men make mistakes, but only fools make the same mistake twice."

That, I have to say, I find not only dreary but absurd. Wise humans, men and women alike—wise and *courageous* humans—dare to make the same mistake not twice, but as many times as it takes to get closer to attaining even the unattainable. You won't ever sprout wings, no, but learning to hang glide is pretty cool.

Do you know what my old brain sees as a big problem with Justice? It's the need for judges that comes along with it. A big problem with judges, of course, is that they're not only not angels, but not even free spirits. They're as governed by human nature as you and I—or at least *you.* Some societies, such as ours, have tried to reduce that problem by having other judges judge the judges, and then having more judges judging *them.* I don't know whether that simply compounds the problem or not, but at least to my judiciously ignorant eye, it doesn't look good when the ultimate arbiters in a society are appointed by the Boss, a Boss who may not even have been elected by the majority of the people in that society in the first place. But who am I either to know or to come up with a better alternative?

I think there's a clue in all this, though. There's been a persistent need among humans to leapfrog all the judges who judge one another as they go about judging us, and to make a final appeal to a Great Judgment Seat in the sky. It seems to me there are two things, apart from its persistence, that are particularly worth noting in the recurring visions of that place up there. The first is that it always sidesteps the issue of human nature and becomes Divine—with a capital D, of course—so that we're not supposed to shoot at it. Its second notable feature is that it's a place of no appeal, no appeal whatsoever. What I find suggestively revealing about that is the way it re-embraces exactly what your human crusade for Justice among yourselves has fought so hard to cast aside. Up there, there's a King of Kings, a Lord of Lords. There's The Master, The Teacher, and let's not overlook The Shepherd, none of whose flock gets so much as a bleating vote. I feel like I'm back at the beginning of the long road again, back to that village by the beach and the justice I saw handed out there. In fact, I'm back even farther, to the human family, aren't I? It's God the Father up there, isn't it? Dad makes the rules, and Dad does the spanking.

I think that deep down inside, that's the way you want it, otherwise we'd be bowing to a The President of Presidents, or a Prime Minister of Prime Ministers. I think you know that while Democracy may seem a better concoction than some other brews, the only recipe for capital-J Justice on this tiny planet, crawling as it is with other humans, calls for a benign and wise dictator who calls the right shots, dispenses just the right amount of freedom, tells you the right things you have to do, and makes the right decisions about what to do about it when you don't do them. Would that be Heaven, or what?

That's exactly what it would be, Heaven. You may or may not think Heaven exists, but it's got a capital H, so don't shoot at it, or you may end up in that other place. By all means go on doing the best you can about liberty and justice, but consider keeping their initial letters small. Our benign dictator has yet to arrive, and whenever he or she shows up, you'll overthrow him or her anyway. You'll once again unfurl the banners of the unattainable Ideals, break out the firearms the Bill of Rights says you can keep under your beds, and take to the barricades. You won't like the benign dictator's absolute authority and power. You'll want some of it, too, *lots* of it, certainly a larger share than your neighbor gets. That's your nature. You're human beings, don't forget. You can't have Heaven on Earth. You can't have your cake and eat it too.

That's another of those dreary and absurd expressions, don't you think? Who's that out there telling me what I can and can't have, anyway? I'm free to eat whatever I want, thank you! Give me cake and then tell me I can't eat it? That wouldn't be fair!

Besides, what do you want me to do with my cake? Polish my car?

Let Me Speak To Your Supervisor!

I'm sitting here writing, trying to stop myself going back to the television set in the other room. An alliance of American and British forces is tightening the noose around Baghdad. Over there, across the world, night is falling, and it will be another night of sun-bright explosions in the darkness, of shrieks from burned and shattered bodies, of the long, patient work of human hands blasted—in half a human second—to rubble and dust. For the people living there, it will be another long night of terror and tears. Daylight will, of course, bring the rising sun to Baghdad, the sun that rises now outside my window beyond the quiet meadow and the glassy pond. It looks still and tranquil out there in my familiar landscape, but there's killing and carnage aplenty going on right before my eyes. I can't see it, though, and I don't care. After all, Nature, by nature, is supposed to be uncivilized, isn't it? It's natural, so why fret about it?

I don't want to keep watching the breaking news in the valley of the Tigris and Euphrates. I seem to remember that in school that valley was called the "cradle of civilization." Today it will be a valley of coffins and grief. On our side of the world, too, the American and British families of the dead and prisoners of war will spend today, and many, many tomorrows, in anguish.

The Flow doesn't care any more about Baghdad than I care about the mayhem in the grass, the murder going on in the water of the pond, or, for that matter, the devastation and obliteration of life my footfalls cause as I walk to my hammock between the trees, which I will surely do later on. The Flow just flows, and bugs and humans go on doing what bugs and humans do, busily killing one another.

One of the things humans do best is being ingenious. I'm truly awestruck, for instance, by the human ingenuity that went into this computer I'm working on. I'm awestruck by the human *me*, by my ingenuity in figuring out the frequent challenges this computer throws my way. These are simple things compared to what the news is showing me right now. Beyond the city of Baghdad, across the land and its borders, out into the waters of the nearby seas, massive deployments of armaments show that there seem to be no limits to what humans can think up. Rough terrain is no problem for these juggernauts. What's more, you've found ways for them to float and fly. You've given them sensors of their own that let them look and hear and feel out their targets. Well, not *their* targets; yours.

You and I aren't dummies, and we know all these inventions took a lot of money. Even though people are always complaining that they haven't enough money to go around, not enough for the mortgage payments, the groceries, the medical bills, someone up there has plenty of it to spend on things like going to Mars and going to Baghdad. Money? It may be hard for you and me to get our hands on, but, hey, every day people are being paid with it to print more of it. Other people are being paid, with as much of it as they ask for, to decide what it should buy. There's always enough money to fund the human drive for power and domination. Funding shelter for the homeless, or care for the sick, or food for the hungry, are low priorities. In a Banana Republic, a banana isn't just a banana.

That's "government" for you, and whenever there's more than one human trying to get something done, there seems to be no way around having such a thing. Put two humans together, and you'll get disagreements over who gets to do what, or what's supposed to get done next. Even in two-person undertakings, one person has to break the deadlocks and make the decisions that keep the ball rolling. Someone has to govern.

Loving couples may be able to compromise over an issue, talk it over and make a joint decision. Even that's iffy. Faced with disagreement, loving couples often stop being so loving, grow cool to one another, cruel to one another, violent and even murderous. That's a tough way to sort things out, to go about "governing," but it sure settles the argument. Ask Anne Boleyn or Catherine Howard. If it can get that bad with only two of you, is it likely to get any better when lots of you get involved? What does common sense tell you is going to happen when you multiply a couple into a family, a family into a neighborhood, a neighborhood into a city . . . and on and on and on until you have the inhabitants of a crowded nation bringing all their various disagreements to the task of decision making?

Let's ratchet the situation up a notch and go international. Why should anyone think there can be peaceful, non-violent, long-lasting solutions to serious, international disagreements? There can't be, not in the long run, because that isn't the way you're made. The microscopic invasions and sieges and counter-attacks that are happening all the time in the human body, among cells and viruses and bacteria, are a telltale clue to the situation. Violence is simply one manifestation of change, and there's no changing the inevitability of change. Killing goes on beneath the microscope in the lab, in the grass of the meadow, beneath the surface of the pond, and wherever humans come together. Somewhere, there will always be dead in the streets.

I wish I could stop you fretting about it. I don't fret about it, not about the fact of the matter, but that's my Flow side showing. Should I fret about the weather? That sometimes it's dry and sometimes wet, sometimes hot and sometimes cold? That's the way it is, and I dress accordingly.

I don't want you to think I'm a callous, cynical old man. If you asked my friends and neighbors if that's what I am, I don't believe they'd say so. It isn't either callous or cynical to accept the ways of change, and with that acceptance comes a release from the fruitless hard labor of pursuing illusion. There's a guy in Greek mythology who had to keep trying to roll a boulder up a hill, a boulder that always rolled back down again before he could get it to the top. Talk about fruitless hard labor! He'd have done better to have looked around at the bottom of the hill and think about how his efforts could be used better. Maybe that boulder could have served to grind corn, or been used as the cornerstone of a building.

Like you, no doubt, I do fret at times. That's my human side showing. But I don't fret about the fact that winter will come. What I fret about is that when winter does come, will there be enough sweaters to go around?

I'm not a disillusioned, disappointed or resigned old person, either. I'm not proposing that newborns in the delivery room, held up by their heels and slapped on the back, be shown a sign—upside down, of course—that says "Abandon hope all ye who enter here." To become disillusioned, I'd have to have had illusions to begin with. To become disappointed, I'd have to have had unrealized hopes and expectations. To become resigned, I'd have to have given up hopes for a fate different than the one I got. I came into the delivery room with none of these things and so was spared the possibility of such gloomy outcomes. I came in already knowing about the immense and impartial flow of things. I arrived knowing about it—and content.

There's a small house in the village that I used to pass often on my way to our recycling center. One day there was a sign planted in the front yard that said, "If life gives you lemons, make lemonade." I liked that sign and wondered who lived there. I never got to meet the person, but the rather disapproving village rumor mill said it was a man who was living with AIDS. After a while, the sign came down, and the house was repainted and sold. The last time I passed the house, which was a while ago because now someone takes my recyclables for me, we were about to have a presidential election. There were signs in lots of the yards urging passers-by to vote for either Gore or Bush. The necessary business of government was at work, but I found myself thinking about the sign to do with lemons instead. That sign might have been something to show newborns in the delivery room. Government, I thought, must have meant little to the man who had put it up, and he, certainly, meant little to government. I hope he had good friends.

I'm rambling, I know, my mind wandering about from Baghdad to illusions to lemonade. But I keep coming back to government, because government seems to be where so many of you put your hopes that human affairs will get better. Human affairs are the way they are because they're human, and so are the games that go on in the arena of government. There's the tendency to give the idea of government some kind of nobility. That, for sure, is flinging wide the doors to disillusion, disappointment and resignation. Government in some form is necessary, yes, but noble, no. It's sort of like brushing your teeth. If you really want to get to a Promised Land in human affairs, a government mass transit system is the last way to get there. You'll do better standing by the side of the road, holding out your thumb.

If you ask me, a noble government here on Earth—not in Heaven—would be under the rule of a prophet, one of those odd humans who personify the kinder sides of human nature. That "wise" person, whose gender would be irrelevant, would call the shots with a firm, loving hand, keeping the necessary compromises fair, so that everyone lost a little now and then in the short run, but gained more than was lost over the long haul. Penalties for not going along with the program would be clear, swift and sure, but they wouldn't be either vindictive or violent. Some players in the game would, for sure, have to spend time in some kind of penalty box, but that box wouldn't look like a wild-animal cage. There would be those who, for some reason, were habitually unable to play the game without committing fouls—after all, we're talking about governing *humans* here, humans with their full range of possibilities. These players might have to be permanently sidelined, not to road gangs and salt mines, but to secure enclaves where they could work out their violence among themselves and apart from the rest. There would be few of them, only those who were genetically predisposed to violence. Our imaginary prophet would have seen to it that violence's swampy breeding grounds—deprivation, abuse and injustice—would have been drained.

Yeah, sure. Maybe on some other planet. That's right, we both know it can't happen here. The arrows of Liberty, Fraternity, Justice and Equality can be notched to the bowstrings of the archers, but we all know what happens to the arrows when they're let loose.

Are all "men" created equal? Apart from its gender problems, it's a fine phrase, and wouldn't it be great if they were? No, they're not created equal, neither all men among themselves, nor all women among themselves, and men and women are certainly not created "equal" among each other. For starters, we're not "created" at all. We happened. Once we did, genes mingled and produced a limitless variety of shapes, sizes and potential capabilities. Equal how? The writers didn't say, but they may have had in mind "equal in the sight of God." In the sight of God is not a good place to turn up expecting to be equal. No one's looking.

Are we all born with the inalienable rights of life, liberty and the pursuit of happiness? I wish for you that it were so, but "rights" aren't part of any genetic package I've heard about. Our inhabitants of Valley A and Valley B weren't born with a little package of undisclosed contents to be opened in the privacy of their own homes. Someone made up rights along the way, and it's always been the strongest among you who have decided what those rights were, and who got any of them.

And yet, in your search for transportation to the Promised Land, you've come up with governments that are supposed to rest on these ideas, to rest on thin air. Governments can't rest on wishful thinking, at least not for long. Governments are heavy things and the force of human nature's gravity is strong. All governments built on ideals beyond human attainment must fall to earth.

I'm in a worse than poor position to conduct a survey of the history of government. I never took so much as a Civics course. I don't remember even being offered one at any of the toney schools I went to. The little bit of history you and I have picked up here and there, and the daily news of the history we've lived through, will have to do.

There seem to have been a good many variations over the years on the "Shut up and do what you're told" theme. We can probably thank the strongest Neanderthal with the biggest club for setting that enduring example. There have been shamans and high priests galore who called the shots, relying on the invisible to give them stature in their communities. Emperors and kings wrote pages of history in the hot, red blood of dissenters, though they didn't always get away with it. The wily and resourceful disobedient sometimes managed to thumb their noses at the royal command, "Off with his head!" and offed the kingpin's head instead. Then, the words of the ongoing historical saga flowed on across the pages in ink that was alleged to be blue.

Along the way there were lots of Councils of Elders—Round Tables and the like. They were supposed to help the Boss Man make wise decisions and keep him from jumping the rails. The trouble was, some of these trusty advisors were always after either The Boss's job or his woman. That's only human nature, isn't it? Whatever it is, it's no way to run a ship unless you're hell-bent on a shipwreck.

Let's see . . . What else? Oh yes, a whole long list of generals have taken a shot at governing, no pun intended. They usually had armies to back them up. Often, they were able to keep the unarmed populace subdued for a while, but common, human sense says you can't have that many side arms walking around in the same palace without a colonel taking a shot at the general.

One of the most ill-fated experiments in government, it seems to me, has been for a small group of strong men to try to run the show together. How on earth could that have been expected to work? No matter how big the turf, or how carefully you divide it up, there's never going to be enough to go around to satisfy everyone. Turf seems as addictive to humans as liquor or cocaine. The more you have, the more you crave. Sooner or later, you've got to get your hands on somebody else's stash, like, for instance, the stash of one of your fellow strong men.

It's only in recent history that someone came up with the radical notion of letting the people govern themselves. It was an off-the-wall idea, but nothing else seemed to have worked, and it tapped into one of human nature's basics. No, I don't think the appeal had to do with lofty ideals, though the idea came wrapped up in that fine paper. I think the appeal was the same, old, familiar one of power. "Power to the people!" sounded good. Were "the people" likely to turn down such an offer? If you were a kid, hanging around waiting for someone to throw you the occasional jelly bean, would you turn down an offer to run the jelly-bean factory? I don't think so.

Someone, of course, had to figure out how to move this new idea of the people governing themselves off paper and into practice. Lots of "someones" did so, and that, in itself, didn't bode well. Bright minds worked hard at it all the same, and they came up with a variety of formulas in a variety of different places. One obvious one that didn't take a lot of figuring was simply to grab the factory by force and promise that everything that came out of it belonged to the people. When the factory sputtered to a halt, the people wanted to know why. In these places, it was back to square one, time to revert to a "Shut up and do what you're told" kind of government. In other places, royalty and such were allowed to stay around, but only to be decorative, uplifting examples to the now-powerful people. Other places did away with royalty altogether and decided to have presidents and prime ministers, answerable to the people through things like parliaments and congresses.

It never became clear where the people's power was actually supposed to reside. Was there really a way for the notion that "the people" were governing themselves to get off the shelf in the store and become a deliverable package of goods? Government *of* the people, *for* the people, and *by* the people? How?

The vote, that's how. The ballot, not the bullet. The people would choose who got to go to the capital and make the laws. That's where the people's power would lie. "The people" would choose? Well, at the beginning, only some of the people. Human nature being what it is, it took a while, and some nasty incidents, for it to dawn on the more powerful of the people—like the visionary intellectuals and the landed gentry with a lot at stake—that "colored" people and "female" people were people, too. I wonder what the Founding Fathers thought they were? What could have been going on under those powdered wigs as the sharp quill pens, held by surprisingly workmanlike fingers, scratched and squiggled across the parchment, again and again, the phrase "the people"? I seem to recall that even when the light bulb went on in that dark room, illuminating *all* people as people, there were still some people who thought that some other people weren't as fully people as they, themselves, were. Everyone should have a vote, they grudgingly agreed, but people like us should get a couple or three. That particular arrow didn't fly at all. Of course not. Those superior people couldn't agree on which of them was more superior than the other.

I vote. Not all the time and every chance I get, but I like feeling part of the game. I vote most regularly at the local level, for village officials and the like. I know who they are and what they've been doing around here. I can, with some confidence, form an opinion about whether or not their ideas make sense, and whether they might be remotely capable of doing what they claim should be done. I even took the trouble to read the village budget once, when there was a hot debate going on about a landfill issue. After a good deal of head-scratching, I could actually understand it.

In the government of our village, I'm completely at ease with what some people call "corruption." I so admire your persistent reach for ideal behaviors far beyond your grasp, but it seems unnecessarily masochistic of you to give human nature a bad rap when it's all you've got to work with. Your strong sense of fairness, for instance, means that favors will get returned. There's nothing about that to deserve the label of corruption. Here in the village, we know why some permits rise to the top of the pile quicker than others, why some variances in the building code are granted and others aren't. It's not bird-brained to feather one's nest when an opportunity occurs, and here, we know why some land deals go one way and not another. Since I've been here, I can't remember anyone's hand being caught in the till, or anyone being accused of stuffing ballot boxes. In our little world, trying to get away with those sorts of capers would be like trying to hide an elephant under a handkerchief. But if you run the Architectural Review Board in your community, and you tilt the balance scale of a decision in favor of your sister-in-law, are you engaging in corruption or upholding the ideal of family loyalty?

I find the phrase "corrupt government" both redundant and unfairly pejorative. Government is always going to be "corrupt" measured by some unattainable standard. It's *how* corrupt it is that counts, what form that corruption takes, how much damage it causes. It's like drinking liquor. The wise drinker knows his or her limits, and we need to remember that Prohibition was another of those arrows that didn't take flight. I like our kind of corruption in village politics. It's human nature right out there in the open, right at eye level.

Thinking about it now, I can see that the further away from home my vote extends, the less I'm inclined to use it. I'm pretty regular on the township level, but I know I slack off when it comes to the county, and my record is, at best, fair-to-middling in state-wide election races. There, I don't know the horses anymore. I'm uncertain about the pros and cons of the issues, and even with a lot of head-scratching, I could never make sense of the budgets. I can't find it in myself to vote a straight ticket just because that's how my family always voted, or because my best friends vote that way. Political platforms are big things, and I've never come across one I could swallow whole. Because of my odd, outsider status among you all, I'm a lot shorter on emotions than you are, and emotions are what seem to make it easier for people to be regular voters.

As you've probably guessed, I have been registering for a long time as an independent. That puts me among the "lesser people" who don't get a vote in the primary elections, which puzzles me, but that's the way it's worked out. If I ran the place, I'd be tempted to give people who thought independently two votes instead of one. As it is, there's never much of an independent platform to think about, and the occasional independent candidate never gets anywhere. But that's okay with me. A strong, independent candidate with a big platform wouldn't be independent anymore, and then I'd have to hunt around for something else to call myself if I wanted to stay in the game.

National elections, I admit, confound me. They must confound a lot of people, because in spite of the vote supposedly being the true expression of their power, so few people bother to use it at the national level. It can end up that the majority that elects the President isn't a majority of the people at all, but only a majority of the half, or even less than half, of the people who bothered to vote. That's not a big vote of confidence, and it perplexes me that politicians seem so quick to skim over that little detail and speak with such certainty about what it is "the American people" want. How can they know, when so few of the people spoke? I'm told that because of the totally mysterious invention called the Electoral College, even if everyone in the country suddenly took it into their heads to flex their muscles, exercise their power, and voted, the winner who got the most votes could actually wind up the loser.

I'd say "Go figure!" but even an amateur observer of human nature, like myself, can figure it out. You've never really thought you were all equal, and you're right. Some of you have always been more capable of doing some tasks than others are, and that's not about to change.

I do remember being taught, back in my school days, that our democratic system of government was noteworthy because it contained a "system of checks and balances." There were three branches of government, as I recall, that were meant to keep an eye on each other. There was the Executive, the Judiciary, and . . . and all the congressional stuff. The Federal branch, was it? What I don't remember being taught was anything about the obvious checks and balances that got placed on the voice of the people. I suppose telling it like it is could have gotten the teacher fired.

Speaking for myself, human governance up there in Washington has become too confusing and convoluted to sort out, has lost its human scale.

Even the inevitable wheelings and dealings aren't at eye-level anymore. There are suggestions that more and more of "we, the people," are feeling skeptical, feeling alienated and powerless, and are drifting away. For me, that's only a matter of interest, not of concern, but for a lot of other people, there's a lot at stake. Fortunately for those with the most to lose, there's a tried-and-true method of countering public doubt when that doubt threatens the system: You herd the people onto the yellow brick road and head for Oz, revving up the engines of mystery and thrusting the people's emotions into high gear.

In the earliest days following the American Revolution, the innovative ideals and ideas were so new and bright and large that they riveted everyone's attention on pie in the sky and obscured the drearier landscape of human nature. There wasn't any need for a whole lot of pomp and ceremony to dress up the new notions. In fact, to have imported all that British pomp and circumstance would have been positively counter-revolutionary. My impression is that the early politicians worked out of taverns and their homes, that George Washington's first presidential residence was a plain kind of place. Pictures suggest the dress code, for civilians and military alike, was neat and tidy, plain and serviceable. From what little I know about it, the music of the time was simple—a couple of fifes, and a couple of drums, and a few basic tunes. Was there a national anthem in the early days? If there was, I don't think I've ever heard it. It certainly can't have been anything like the complicated one that blesses baseball games.

There were stirring words in the air, to be sure, words to match the stirring ideas, but I like to think they were measured, practical, utilitarian words, words without mystery, words that got to the heart of the matter, words like "No taxation without representation." The new ideas gave the words their ability to stir, not the other way around. These were not mysterious and emotional words, purposefully orchestrated to stir up support for ideals without merit.

When it came time to bring the pie in the sky down to earth, though, and make it the people's daily diet, there were problems, human problems. Who should cut the pie, and into how many pieces? Who should get the pieces? Oh dear. Enter the doubts. All right, then, counter the doubts. Head for Oz. Build a white palace, smarten up the uniforms. Consecrate the flag. Give it a name, a name that resounds—how about Old Glory?—and send out a decree that it should never be allowed to be soiled by touching *terra firma*. After all, that's solid ground. And O ye composers, come up with, or appropriate if you have to, a repertoire of new music! You know, rousers like "My country 'tis of Thee," "America the Beautiful," "The Battle Hymn of the Republic," "Hail to the Chief!" Wordsmiths to your pens! Give us new words that can make us brave, bring tears to our eyes! So, okay, we've found some glitches with our ideas and ideals, so we'd better have a Pledge of Allegiance. What we need, above all, are words that can make the doubters among us feel small and unworthy in their doubting.

Now here's a project for young, budding scholars who haven't made up their minds what to do for a thesis: Map out the decline of that early ideological certainty as it descends into the quicksand of practicality and compromise. Compare the line it makes on a graph with another line that charts the rise of "theater"—the creation of "Government, the musical." Any correlation? No? Oh well, I still like the idea.

You know what? If I were that guy who's made billions (or is it zillions by now?) with his computers, I'd fund a place on the Internet where everyone could regularly register their opinion about national issues with a couple of taps on a keyboard. I'd be like Andrew Carnegie and his libraries, and bring keyboards within reach of everyone's fingers—yes, *all* of the people's fingers. I'd make keyboards more commonplace than television sets. Then, politicians might be justified in talking about what the American people want.

What a blow to the notion of "equality" that would be! What an assault on democracy, on government of, for, and by the people! "The people's" emotions would be right out there, a large majority perhaps calling for a war or, on the other hand, for the defense budget to be cut in half. A majority might log on for an end to all taxes, or perhaps voice an opinion that not a penny should be spent on any of the arts, or that all health care should be free. Or that all people of color should go back to wherever they came from. Human nature's human nature. Why, 95 percent of all Texans might vote to secede and have their own country. Self-determination is a great idea, but not within *this* Union, thank you very much. This Union's sacred.

At that point, the few, who thought they were more enlightened than the rest, would have to step in. They'd justify ignoring the people's voice by saying they had more education about these matters, more information—classified, or course—, a broader viewpoint, more experience in such things—all of which might be true. But the curtain in front of the altar for government of, for, and by the people would be whisked away, revealing the Wizard of Oz as naked as a jaybird.

I hear the Internet is moving in that direction, and that there are worried people in Washington. If I were in Washington, and wanting to stay there for a while, I'd be worried, too. I'd be worried about my own future, of course, but what would keep me awake at night would be knowing that even after more than 200 years, this democratic society is a fragile thing, as fragile but as heavy as fired clay, and that it's kept aloft only by smoke, mirrors, sleight of hand, and wishful thinking.

If I were a betting man, I'd bet that the Internet *will* come to be a serious threat to the power brokers. I'd bet that ways *will* be found to curb its awesome potential. I'd bet that wily filters will slip in between the governors and the governed, and that the governors will, of course, always prevail. In other words, I'd bet on human nature continuing to be being what it is. And I bet I'd win my bet. I won't be around to collect, of course, but you may live to see the outcome. I think you're in for a wild ride, and I'm sorry I won't be on the roller coaster with you.

Now I can't resist any longer. I have to go back to the TV and see what's becoming of the cradle of civilization.

How Do I Know?

I'm worrying that at times my voice may be sounding teachy or preachy to you. I don't ever want it to sound that way, but I guess there's not much chance it won't. You see, there *is* something I know that you don't, and I want—passionately—for you to have this knowledge that I have. I *know* that what you do here with your life has no meaning other than the one you choose to give it while you're here, and other than the effect of your choices on your fellow human beings.

"How do I know?" I hear you ask.

Now *there's* a fine example of the banana skins that words slip under our feet! When you read that question—and did you pronounce that "reed" or "red"?—I wonder on which word your mind put (or, depending, puts) the emphasis. I wonder if your inner voice went (goes?) up or down at the end.

One short sentence. Four little words, none more than four letters. Unspoken, we've got a mixed green salad of possible meanings on our hands. Spoken aloud to one another in person, we'd at least have some salad dressing to help us—the oil and vinegar of the lilt of the voice, the movements of eyebrows, shoulders and hands. I might shift uncertainly from buttock to buttock. You might cross your legs complacently, or, on the other hand, uncross them and lean forward in emphasis. If we were talking together on a beach, the nervous wiggling of my toes might tip you off that I wasn't as sure of myself as I sounded. But though I like to imagine you sitting over there, I know we're invisible to one another. I know that, because I can't see you, and I can see the chair is empty. I know the words lie flat and silent on the page, and how I meant you to read them is up for grabs.

You get the point. The point? I can't even know which point you got, or even if you got one at all. How do I know?

Sitting here as often as I do these days, trying to find ways to talk to you so that you'll understand, I've gotten used to floundering about. This evening, it seems I'm destined to flounder about in a mixed green salad. "Flounder?" That's just given me a good idea. I'm going to stop the music I'm listening to—some fusion jazz I like—and put on a recording of humpback whales talking to each other. That way, I can wonder what they're talking about, while you wonder what I'm trying to say. You and I will sort of be in sync.

It may be that we're sunk already, but never mind. Come join me in my salad and flounder for a while.

"HOW do you know?"

If your voice went up when you read that heading, I'm inclined to answer your question with an "I know because . . ." kind of response.

"*How* do you know she's cheating on her husband?"

"I know, because I'm the guy she's cheating with."

I know first hand. I know from experience. That's the way all of us come to think we know a lot of the things we think we know, isn't it? First-hand experience is a form of education we all get, whether we like it or not. It's guaranteed to last a lifetime, and it's free. What a deal! Have we really hit upon the lunch that *is* free? Where's the catch?

The catch is this: The only item on the free-lunch menu is the catch of the day, and it's always the same. What we learn about things from first-hand experience is more about ourselves, about our individual natures, than it is about the nature of the things themselves.

Can we agree that, as someone said, "Water will certainly wet us, and fire will certainly burn"? No, we can't even do that. Water *can* certainly wet us and fire *can* certainly burn us, but neither is inevitable. It depends on us. It depends on whether we forgot our umbrella, or if we ignored our parents' stern caution not to play with matches. When I get wet or get burned, it tells me that I'm forgetful, or careless or stupid, or, as is often the case, all three. I don't know what first-hand experience tells you about honesty, but it tells me that honesty is *not* always the best policy. Pleading guilty, even when you are, can land you in a heap of trouble you may not deserve. White lies and half truths make the world go 'round. And while we're talking about the world going around, first-hand experience tells me the Earth is flat and the sun comes up and the sun goes down. Anyone with eyes to see knows that's so, right? Those freaks who tell us we're spinning in circles and swinging through space at dizzying speeds? They've got to be kidding!

First-hand experience is unreliable stuff. What it is is only such experience as the human mechanism can process, and to make things worse, each human has a different configuration of cogs and wheels.

If, on the other hand, your voice went down when you asked *"How do I know?"* I'd be inclined to start telling you about neurons firing and synapses doing whatever it is that synapses do. I'd launch into an explanation of how the five senses work. My launch would be about as successful as that of the ship, dripping with champagne, that slid down the rails of the shipyard and sunk beneath the waves without a trace. I haven't the faintest idea how such things work.

"How DO you know?"

Ask me that with a rising voice, and I'll assume you really think I do know something. Let your voice fall, and the whole matter is in doubt.

"How do YOU know?"

With an upward lilt, I hear you asking me why I'm in the privileged position of knowing something other people don't. Maybe experience or circumstance has blessed me with information unavailable to others. Maybe *I* know that it's possible to walk across red-hot coals in bare feet because I've seen someone do it. Yeah, well . . . . And should you believe me?

"How do you KNOW?"

Up goes your voice, because my certainty has come on as relentless as a steamroller. Whatever it is, I don't just think it's so, or opine that it's so, or even believe it's so. I claim out-and-out that I *know* it's so. Naturally, there's something you'd like to know, too, like what the source of my certainty is. I may tell you that it comes from my own first-hand experience. I hope that's what I'll say, because I find that delusional certainty a common, natural one and easy to let slide by. It's going to be harder for you if I tell you I heard whatever it is from someone I trust, even if it came from *that* person's first-hand experience. In my first-hand experience, those are not usually the answers people usually give, though. I've come to expect dreaded answers like, "I read it in the newspaper," or "I saw it on TV," or the one that's supposed to clinch everything: "I heard it on Public Radio."

Ah, yes, "the media," upon which we rely for so much of the information that congeals in our heads into what we think is knowledge. Many of us pride ourselves on being selective about where in the media we turn for our information. My friends nowadays are a different breed from the beloved, reckless buddies of my youth. Back then, the only outside input they considered trustworthy was whatever agreed with their passionate, radical, anti-establishment notions. These days, for the most part, my friends are smart, well-educated, seasoned, rational people. I have to say they're not as much fun as my buddies of yore, but, hey, they're old. Some of them can pass as wise. They select their media input carefully. They consider trustworthy only what agrees with their thoughtful, middle-of-the road, stay-within-the-system notions—the notions they've come to hold from first-hand experience. They're careful to trust only media input that comes from reliable sources.

Are these sources reliable? Just listen to my voice drop an octave at the end when I answer, "How do I *know*?"

Enough floundering about. I'm ready to find some solid ground beneath this tossed salad, but the trouble is, there doesn't seem to be any there. And yet, it seems to me that when it comes to *knowing* things, building solid ground to stand on was what "education" was supposed to be all about.

My education, like yours, began in the delivery room. We could go back even further to the moment of conception, but that's opening another can of worms, and we don't need more worms in this salad. I'm going to leave those worms tightly packed in their amniotic fluid, dormant in the darkness of their well-padded container. Arbitrary as it may be, I'm going to say that our first-hand experiences kicked in under the bright lights of the delivery theater, when we were pushed and pulled onto stage center before an audience full of eager anticipation.

That is, the audience was full of eager anticipation *if we were lucky*. If we weren't, we had to start our performance amidst catcalls and a hail of rotten eggs and tomatoes. Stage center is a tricky place to have to make a public debut, especially when we haven't the faintest idea what we're supposed to be doing there. All we can do is try to please the audience, relying on the first-hand experience of trial and error to teach us how to do that. Sometimes we can't get laughter or applause, no matter what we come up with. But the show must go on. It may be that all we can do until the day the curtain falls, sometimes mercifully, is dodge the missiles and hide behind the available scenery. Or, we might manage to learn some quick alchemy, transforming the eggs and tomatoes into guns and knives and Molotov cocktails . . . and strike back.

I wonder what your public debut was like, what kind of play you found yourself starring in, and in front of what kind of audience. I wonder what your earliest first-hand experiences taught you about what kind of performance you were there to give. How do *I* know? (Falling voice.) I don't, of course. I can't. What I *think* I know, though, is that the answers would be different for each of us. For each of us, our earliest first-hand experiences would have revealed a different play in progress around us.

New metaphor, mixed recklessly with the previous: If you and I were able to compare the scripts of our plays, we might discover some common ground to stand on. But *solid* common ground? I certainly don't think it would be solid enough to hold up the kind of structure we might want to build—a structure we could both comfortably inhabit.

I know: This metaphor is getting completely out of hand, but try to stick with me for a moment. To begin with, we'd each bring different foundation materials to the task. They'd lend themselves to structures of different sizes, shapes and composition. They'd predetermine buildings of different designs, different heights and breadths, different square footage. Even if our earliest first-hand experiences did happen to bring us compatible building materials to work with, we'd work with them, fashion them, differently. As we went about our joint construction tasks, far from finding our common ground solid, we'd find it shifting beneath our feet.

Be all that as it may, out we go, out of the delivery room and into the home. Out of the frying pan and into the fire. We're still a soft little thing, old enough, perhaps, to be a bit confused, but that's what families are for: to unconfuse us. Mom and Dad may have different ideas about how to do that, but what can you expect when their own common ground is shaky, too, about as solid as a waterbed! Good old water! It can be a metaphor for everything, and I'm not going to pass up the chance, never mind that I began this paragraph with fire. Once we're at home, more first-hand experiences pour in, not in trickles, but in torrents and floods. Each of us finds our own way to stay afloat. It may be by hailing a passing yacht, or it may be by building our own little kayak, or it may be by hanging, white knuckled, onto a log. But afloat we are—that is, if we're still alive.

Lucky I mentioned logs. It's grown chilly here in my den, as you may have noticed, and it's time for me to put another log on the fire. I don't really need to. I could turn up the thermostat. I could save money on wood and spend it on oil. Wood's getting expensive. Logs aren't what they used to be—hefty and dry and long-lasting. A cord of wood doesn't seem to be what it used to be, either. I ordered a cord this fall, and, with a straight face, they brought me what they called a "face cord." There was half as much wood as I expected, and it seems to burn twice as fast as it used to. The only thing that's stayed the same is the price. How reassuring to find there are things you can count on! At least until next year.

While we're on the subject of fire, I wonder what your first-hand experiences told you about it. Mine bring me a rush of pleasant associations. The first that comes to my mind is my father telling me stories beside the fireplace before I had to go to bed. That makes me think of campfires and marshmallows, which is pleasant, even though I hated being sent to a summer camp. One year—I must have been about ten—my parents tried to turn me into a Boy Scout, complete with uniform and all. By then, I already knew I was different, and I couldn't buy into the Boy Scout oaths and such. I didn't mind the idea of pledging to be honest, or to do a good deed every day, but to me, even at that age, honesty and goodness were only human options, not some kind of universal ultimates. I had no ultimates, because I knew there were none. I knew the universe didn't care if I were honest and good, rather than devious and malevolent. I already knew the universe didn't "care" about anything.

As you can imagine, my Scouting experience was short-lived. One day, I came across a squirrel that had been horribly mutilated by some predator, or perhaps, who knows, by a man-made trap. It was still alive, but it was obviously beyond repair or recovery. I did the only thing I could think of and stomped on its head. I was caught in the act by a fellow Scout, the idol of our Troop, who was way ahead of the rest of us in ribbons and badges. He turned me in to the Scout Master, who was horrified and thought I should have brought the squirrel back for treatment. Who was I, he asked me, to take the life of one of God's creatures? I knew what I was supposed to say, but at the same time, wasn't I supposed to be honest? I answered that there wasn't a God, and that I thought I'd done a good deed. That put an end to my Boy Scout education.

Thinking back, the only unpleasant association I can remember with fire is a recurrent nightmare I had for a while as a child—a nightmare in which I was always about to be burned at the stake. It must have come from someone telling me about Joan of Arc, or perhaps it was about those unfortunate churchmen in England. Yes, I think it must have been about them, because

I remember feeling quite confused about their being considered the fortunate ones. They were allowed to pack gunpowder under their armpits so they'd blow up fast, rather than burn down slowly. Whoever thought up that small mercy should have been awarded a nifty Scouting badge for having done such a good deed!

Being burned at the stake, packed with gunpowder or not, is a first-hand experience with fire I can do without, thank you very much. If it had happened to me early in life, why, I might never have liked fire again.

My little fire here in my den is crackling along nicely now. The humpback whales are still singing to one another on my CD player, and though I still have no idea what they're singing about, they're lovely songs. The notes that came with the recording tell me that the songs are probably about sex. I guess we and whales aren't as different as we look. I think maybe their songs are about the virtues of burning wood rather than oil. Whales haven't had good first-hand experiences with people who like to burn oil.

I'm cozy here in my den, and I'd like to go on talking to you for a while, but I'm getting sleepy. If you'll excuse me, I think I'll move over into that "distressed" recliner by the fire and just doze off for a bit instead. Besides, I've totally lost my train of thought.

*　　*　　*

It's a little after dawn now. From the look of it, we're in for a cold, gray day. My nap went and turned itself into a night's sleep. It's not the first time. Nowadays, if I don't make the heroic effort to get upstairs to bed when I get sleepy, I don't get there at all. It wouldn't matter, except that when I wake up, I have to spend the next hour or so in the shape of a piece of furniture.

Looking back over what I wrote last night, I'm not surprised I lost my train of thought. That train was rambling about the countryside, laying tracks as it went. If I were a writer, I suppose I'd go back and straighten it all out. But I'm not a writer, thank heavens, so I don't have to bother. Besides, you, my passenger—if you're still aboard, and if you don't mind going from Boston to San Francisco via Alice Springs—can get on and off whenever you like.

What I was doing my best to suggest to you, before I dozed off, was that we need to be wary, even downright distrustful, of turning our individual, first-hand experiences into knowledge we can expect everyone else to share. Whatever information we get from a first-hand experience has to pass through the prism of all our unique, previous experiences, and our past history puts facets on our individual prisms that are as unique as our fingerprints. As for the information that comes to us second-hand, from other people's first-hand experiences, oh my! That information had to pass through *their* uniquely faceted prisms before it got to ours!

Let's have a total fantasy for a moment—the fantasy that we all were faceted alike, that we all came into the delivery room with the same packet of givens, and that we all shared the same first-hand experiences. In such a fantasy, would we then see things the same way? Perhaps we would, but, alas, our common ground would still be as shaky as before. That's because no matter how it was that we both saw and understood things, it would only be the way humans *can* see and understand things. And believe me, there's a lot more going on "out there" than humans will ever be able to perceive.

Like everyone else who goes to school, I took my individual prism of past, first-hand experiences with me—my view of the world as shaped by everything I'd encountered since my debut under the bright lights of the delivery room. I also took along my pencil box, a pencil sharpener, my notebook, and whatever other, tried-and-true, knowledge-capturing utensils that were on the list of items my parents had been told to give me. Looking back now, I think we'd all have done better taking along butterfly nets instead. That's only my view, of course, the view I have from my peculiar perspective. I wasn't fully aware yet of how different I was, certainly not that first morning at Adams Country Day. All of us minnows probably felt odd and uncomfortable in our new aquarium. It was only after we came to feel at home there, secure with the routines and expectations, that I began to sense that something was awry.

In my coloring book, I color-crayoned all the spaces that *weren't* within the lines. The teacher, Miss Bryant, patiently explained that I was supposed to do it the other way around. I couldn't see the sense of that. The pictures the lines made were obvious, so why bother with them anymore? It was what was outside the lines that turned me on. I wasn't a troublemaker, so I did what Miss Bryant asked.

We of course learned basic arithmetic. I thought numbers were fun to work with, but I felt sorry for them. They always had to do the same thing and end up with the same results. I wanted to let them loose to do anything they wanted. On one of my early sheets of simple addition problems, I told the numbers they could add up to anything they wanted to. Three plus three became threes that ran across the page, sometimes shape-shifting into eights along the way. Sixes and nines looked playful to me, so I let them stand on their heads whenever they felt like it.

I can't remember the arithmetic teacher's name, but she asked me to stay after class. Bless her heart, she wasn't angry about my letting my numbers let off steam. She told me that numbers were beautiful because they were predictable, and nothing much else in this world was. I wonder what words she found back then to get her idea across. I don't think I could have known a word like "predictable" yet. Something she said stayed with me. She said, "Treat numbers right, and they'll become your friends." After that, I did treat numbers the way I was supposed to, but the teacher was wrong. First my numbers became boring, and then they became ornery. I still think they resented my putting them back in jail again.

Reading came easily to me. My father read to me almost every night. I was exhilarated to find, little by little, that I could read a story for myself, set off on a fresh hike through new territory whenever I wanted. If the path turned out to be tedious, I could stop and set off in a new direction. For a while, I'd choose anything that could remotely be called science fiction, any fantasy that had anything to do with life "out there." There wasn't a lot of that for early readers, but there was some. In one story I remember, a cat went off on a rocket to the moon. He went hoping to find a whole new world of mice, because he'd heard the moon was made of green cheese. All he found when he got there was a giant, mean, potato bug with whom he had to do battle before rocketing off back to Earth.

Once I could read just about anything, I lost interest in space fantasies. Not one writer seemed able to think up anything totally new. Everything, all the monsters, all the technology, was nothing more than already-known elements of life on Earth, transformed and recombined. In that sense, many of the tales were certainly creative, but they never managed to get me to where I seemed to feel I needed to go. Why was that, I wondered? Now I know it was—and is—because humans wrote the stories, and the human mind can't get outside itself. It's both prisoner and jailer at the same time.

Learning to write was a miserable experience. I don't remember having any trouble learning my letters, or how they went together into words, or how the words went together into sentences, paragraphs and pages. That wasn't the source of my misery. What I couldn't seem to do was get the words to say what I was thinking. No matter how I tried to put the words together, they always ended up telling their reader something different than what I'd asked them to say.

As you can see, some things haven't changed, have they? What has changed, however, is how I feel about it. I don't feel frustrated anymore. Words won't ever tell you what I want to tell you, and I feel okay about that now, because I know they can't. Even a Master's brushstrokes won't enable you to taste the fruit and cheese and wine in a still-life painting. All a painting can do is evoke a sense of something. That's all that words can do, too.

Once I got the hang of school, it was a good place to be. You did what you were supposed to, the way you were supposed to do it, and so long as you did, you got to enjoy all the fun stuff that's called "extra-curricular." My little bit of long-ago Latin tells me that it's called "extra" because it's outside of most formal, required curriculums. Or is that supposed to be *curriculi?* I think, maybe, *curricula.* It's been too many years for me to remember, and there are too few left for me to care.

Even at the posh, respected boarding school where I wound up, the "extra" seemed to mean incidental. We had to pass exams in sociology, but living it out—out there on the playing fields, where the relationship between self and others was the name of the game—that was extra. We had to pass exams in Shakespeare, but The Dramatic Society, supposedly devoted to re-enactments of the ongoing human drama, Shakespeare's included, that was extra, too. I don't remember anything in the curriculum to do with art, or music or dance—such basic expressions of the human being. Possibly there were so-called "electives," I don't know.

Besides The Dramatic Society, there were societies that catered to almost any interest you could think up—a stamp-collecting society, for instance, and a model-airplane society. But there was neither a course nor a society for what interested us most in those days: sex. It wouldn't have been tolerated, of course. Nonetheless, we had to pass rigorous exams in Biology. The closest we came to being taught anything about sex was the day we dissected a frog's reproductive system. We got no help where we really needed it: We were left to ourselves to figure out the hows and whys of making out in the back seat of a car. That was definitely extra, and frogs would have found it easier to do than we did.

Finally, it all made sense to me. Not the making out in the car; I mean the nature of formal education. It was a utilitarian thing, and it was, indeed, useful. I, alone, seemed to know that the "knowledge" we were acquiring was limited, *human* knowledge, knowledge of what humans were capable of knowing. I was awed by how far the human mind was able to push towards its limits, and awed still more by the urge that made it keep on pushing. I'm still in awe today of both the push and the distance gained. There's such a vast amount of human knowledge available that a person has to specialize in ever-smaller bits of it in order to gain mastery of any part, let alone push that little part closer to its own limits.

But the word "vast" is relative, isn't it? It depends on what size you are—or, perhaps, on what size you *think* you are. On that matter, I kept my mouth shut.

I almost came to grief in college when, in my senior year, I opted for a course in comparative religions. Yes, it was extra; it was an elective. It gives me pause to think that all my way through my formal education, which was as good as money could buy, no institution of learning that I attended had, in its *required* curriculum, courses on either of those two constants of human experience—sex and religion. Has there ever been an era or a society without sex? Has there ever been an era or a society without religion? And the two are so closely interwoven, given that it's usually religion that lays down the law about what we're supposed to do with our sexuality. What's more, the two together must account for the lion's share of the blood that's been shed throughout human history and that goes on spilling out today. The lion's share? I can see the lions smacking their lips in their cages under the Coliseum as they catch a whiff of some Christian blood.

Wouldn't you think a useful education ought to include some insight into the age-old, ever-present, human propensity to murder one another? I would. Where would a teacher have to turn for course material? Inevitably, to sex and religion—two components of human-ness as basic as blood and bones. These days, a teacher would only be fired for teaching sex and religion. In the old days, he or she could have been set on fire instead, dispatched to join the enlightened company of the dead. I wonder if having tenure back then included, as an added benefit, an armpit full of dynamite.

Not that any of this matters in the grand scheme of things, because it doesn't. From your point of view, though, I would have thought this perpetual carnage would seem enough of an inconvenience to merit a second look. If I were paying something like $30,000 a year for a university education that claimed it would lead me out of ignorance into wisdom about my world, I think I'd deserve, at the least, a course called Violence 101.

When I signed up for it, I thought the course in comparative religions would have to address the larger question of what religion was and why it came to be. It didn't. It turned out to be one of those so-called "survey" courses. It required us to learn the belief systems of the major religions it covered, and it required our being able, on the final exam, to regurgitate who believed how about what. The "why?" of it all was conspicuously absent.

We were given a choice of subjects for the final essay. I chose one that asked for an analysis of the formative role of growing scientific knowledge as it impacted the different cultures and their beliefs. I'd learned the essay technique of grabbing ahold of a small piece of a large question like that and using it to structure the greater discussion. As I prepared to tackle this science versus religion topic, I chose "Miracles" as my starting point.

As I recall, the point I tried to make was that inexplicable phenomena that religions classify as true miracles are only manifestations of the natural interactions of the human brain with the natural workings of the universe—interactions that the human mind has yet to understand. As scientific knowledge grew, things like eclipses, miraculous events in so many cultural contexts, stopped being miracles. Miraculous visions and miracle cures, I argued, appeared to be miracles to many people only because so little was known about how the human brain works.

Setting up my premise meant establishing its context, attempting to set the miniscularity of human potential against the backdrop of the infinite potential of "The Flow." I ran out of time just as I was warming up to my subject. I got a D—the only one I ever got in all of my school days. On my paper the professor wrote: "You're supposed to be a Senior. This is sophomoric. If you're going to write an essay on The Universe, at least say so. I'd still have given you a D—for not sticking to the point."

I could have kicked myself afterwards. I'd been through enough formal education by the time I was a Senior in college to know that my task was simply to come up with the answers that were considered correct.

Who was the great teacher who gathered his pupils around under a tree and taught them to ask the right questions? Socrates, wasn't it? That reminds me; I just got a guilt-inducing, third request from my old college to contribute to their multi-million-dollar building campaign. Should I suggest they plant a few trees instead? Hell, no! I may be too far beyond their reach for them to give me another D, but they might send the hemlock squad after me. They'll have to hurry if they want to get me. The last train is already pulling into the station, and I'm right here, ticket in hand, ready to get aboard.

What I might do is suggest that when the wise pundits at my old college build their new classrooms, they shape all the ceilings like the inside of the human skull. That special curvature would be a reminder that for all the awesome advancements of knowledge, whatever passes from teacher to student is only a tiny little perspective on a much greater whole, and it's a perspective seen through many, many prisms. Humility—that's what I'd give you if I could. I don't need to give you pride. You've got that already, and quite rightly so. You should be proud, very proud, of all the constructions you've come up with to explain the human phenomenon. *I'm* proud to have been among you, to have been—almost—one of you.

It's your sense of context I fret about. I wish you could try feeling small for a change, as small as anything can be. No matter how small you might imagine yourself, though, you're even smaller than that. You need one another, if you're going to get by amidst the whirling explosions of space. You need each other's visions. You need comfort from one another. You need to give one another meaning, significance. Nothing else will, because there's nothing else that can.

Nothing? *Nothing.*

How do I *know*? (Rising voice.) I *know* it, rather than merely believe it, because the knowledge came with me as surely as the knowledge of how to breathe. I don't believe I breathe, I know I do, and you know that you do, too. In that we're alike. Where we part company is over what it is that we know we breathe. We'd agree we both breathe the air of this planet, but I know I breathe something more. With every single breath I take, I inhale the eternal matter of the stars, of all the suns and planets that come and go, of all the cosmic dust that drifts between. Space, which you see as empty, fills my lungs and seeps through every cell.

It's true for you, too, but that knowledge won't come from formal education, and certainly won't come from the deceptions of first-hand experience. Yes, I wish—passionately—that I could give you this knowledge, but I sit here defeated. I know I can't. All I can do is leave it behind as I go.

SEX

A ha! *That* made you sit up a little straighter in your comfy chair now, didn't it? Of course it did. Sex, among humans, takes precedence. But, oh! the elaborate and ingenious efforts you make to keep it out of sight, where, of course, it refuses to stay put. Well, not "refuses," because that would suggest it had an option, which of course it doesn't. Sex has no intelligence—not even in the case of those school buddies I can remember, who seemed to keep their brains in their Jockey shorts. But I shouldn't let myself be sexist about sex. In the co-ed college I went to, there wasn't any shortage of females who seemed to keep their brains tucked into brief panties, an eye winking naughtily behind a filmy eye patch.

Sex *can't* be confined, because it isn't a separate thing, like a single mouse you can put in a cage. By the way, don't be surprised if you see a mouse scurry across my floor while you're here. They've become bold lately and take me for granted. I gave up setting traps for them when I realized trapping single mice wasn't going to do anything to trap the essence of "mouseness." This is a mousy place out here in the country. I guess that's because mice like sex as much as humans do. Or is it the other way around?

Although the phrase "the birds and the bees" is beating about the bush, I like it. It suggests there's something universal about sex—at least about that little part of that little word that has to do with procreation. Making babies, however, is only one part of the picture; sex has lots of possible outcomes. All the same, acknowledging that the birds and the bees also "do it" acknowledges that sex isn't just some nasty characteristic of the human species.

My vantage point gives me a wide view of this sex business. I know that sex is a glimpse of The Flow flowing, as it does, through all things. I know that only humans, because of their nature, classify and categorize, approve or stigmatize, sex's many different aspects. Humans, of course, don't agree how to do so, any more than they agree about anything else. In fact, when it comes to sex, you humans seem to agree less than you do about lots of other things that are much more complicated, such as the behavior of sub-atomic particles, for instance. You're sort of like the blind men groping the elephant, except that a lot of you seem to be stumbling over each other somewhere between the animal's hind legs.

Sex is a big thing, much bigger than a whole herd of elephants. The human mind interprets it as an urge, an urge that appears to have come tucked in whatever packet of "givens" we arrived with at birth. At least most of us arrived with it. I've met a couple of people along the way who didn't seem to have been given that given, just as I've met others who apparently missed out on the ability to distinguish musical tones or variations in color the way most of us can. I see you squinting at me. I know, I've just compared an urge with an ability, and, yes, I agree that the urge to have sex and the ability to carry out the urge are certainly two different things. I'll stick by the comparison I made anyway, because my point was that nobody's packet of givens contains *all* human possibilities. I, for one, didn't get a sense of direction (as well as a lot of other things). I can pull into a gas station, fill up, and head back the way I came without realizing it. I have no idea which way is which when I come up out of a subway in a city. I didn't, even in the days when I was young and took my urge to a city looking for sex.

The same old English friend who railed against all the *ifs* people used told me a joke, way back when, that I liked enough to still remember. It seems there was this elderly Lord Somebody-or-other who woke up one morning with what we used to call a "stiffie." It was his first in a long time.

"Beasely!" he shouted to his trusty manservant, "Look! I've got an erection!"

"Brilliant, m'lord!" said Beasely. "Shall I inform her Ladyship?"

"Good heavens, no!" said the Lord. "Find me a pair of baggy pants, and we'll smuggle it up to London!"

I think we can agree that part of "sex" is an urge, can't we? We can probably agree, too, that it's not just any old urge, like the urge to travel or meet new people. It's an *urgent* urge that doesn't like taking no for an answer. In fact, it hates being denied so much that it will dissemble, take on disguises, become that favorite of science-fiction writers, the shape-shifter. Talk about a wolf in sheep's clothing! Why, sex can even masquerade as the most innocent of urges, like, for instance, the urge to travel and meet new people. To my way of thinking, it's a "drive" rather than an urge, and I'd ask those psychologists and such in the back row to please put their hands down. Let's not split hairs.

I'm a laymen here, talking about getting laid, and I'm doing the best I can with the words I've got.

As sex drives us along, it has to be driving us *somewhere*. There's a destination, and if you ask me, that somewhere in question is pleasure. I see the hands in the back row fly up again. Yes, I know, on an academic level it may be driving us to make babies and assure the continuation of the species, but first things first: The ecstasy of slobbery kisses, foreplay and orgasms is, in my opinion, this drive's primary destination. For chocoholics, it's the savor of the chocolate that counts, not what happens in the bloodstream afterwards. If procreation were sex's primary destination, then why is my cousin, who's had a vasectomy, hornier than ever? He tells me that it's precisely because the chance of continuing the species is no longer there. He and his wife can get on with it spontaneously, without fumbling about for protective devices. Drive on! Drive faster!

And how about my own delight when I discovered jerking off? My urgent delight! My compulsive delight! There was no question of making babies then, because it was still a dry pleasure, but, man, did it ever feel good! Remember those little gismos you could wind up and hide in the palm of your hand, startling a friend with an "electric" buzz of a handshake? That's how my first orgasms felt—as though my whole body had been buzzed. In my case, that sensation wasn't Nature just giving me a taste of the goodies, so that I'd go on wanting more once my body developed enough to make babies. I had an intuition early on that, being what I am, the ability to procreate was something else, besides a sense of direction, which had been left out of my givens. Did nature throw the switch and turn me off? Hell, no! If babies were where Nature was driving me, then she had no sense of direction, either. But she knew where she was going, all right. She still knows, and she's still at the wheel. These days, I confess, I sometimes feel like Moses being driven to The Promised Land in an old clunker that won't make it that far. Or like Miss Daisy in the back seat, with some crazed teenager under that chauffeur's cap.

Yes, I think pleasure is where sex is driving us. Sadly, for some people that pleasure turns out to be a mirage and shape-shifts into humiliation and pain. There's a lot of horsepower—*bull*power—under the hood of this sexmobile, and it can get out of hand. No culture has found an effective governor to put on that roaring engine. All the rococo constructions of morals and ethics, rewards and punishments that humans have tried haven't worked any better in reining in sex than gossamer threads would work in holding back the rising and setting of the sun.

This beast we're groping is huge, its shade stretching beyond the horizon. We're born in its shadow, grow in its shadow, play and work there, age there. It's only in the last years of a long life that we may—*may*—finally move beyond that shadow's edges into a landscape that is sexually tranquil, a landscape illuminated with a warm glow from a different source. Is that why we call them "the golden years"? It's an optimistic phrase, of course. For many, those golden years are more like rusty iron than gold, and that landscape can be a wintry place, illuminated, if at all, by no more than the pale and distant stars.

I wonder how much older I'd have to get to reach sexual tranquility. I'm fortunate in that these, my waning years, are gilded ones for sure. I do my waning amidst friendships, material comforts, and reasonable health, and I have yet to lose the itch of the urgent drive or the pleasure of scratching it. I don't think that's going to change, because there's not much older for me to get. I hope to die, to leave you and rejoin The Flow, with my pedal to the metal, at the climax of a wet dream, hollering, "I'm coming! I'm coming!" My friends at my bedside will wonder: Did a loved one called him from the "other side"? Only the mortician will know the simple, sticky truth.

That truth *is* simple—and sticky, too, but sticky as in "sticky wicket." Like you do with so many other simple things, though, you all have gone and complicated sex in order to try to understand it, the way you try to pigeonhole everything. All birds don't fit in pigeon holes, and most certainly not the bird of paradise that is an orgasm. Does it matter where it flies or where it comes to roost? Not to The Flow, it doesn't, not a bit. How you "get off," with whom—of which gender or age—, or with what—animal, vegetable or mineral—, or with nothing but fantasies you wouldn't even tell your best friend, couldn't matter less. Not, that is, to The Flow.

The drive to pleasure drives on, regardless, moving along more roads than you will ever map, roads that lead to new destinations in every succeeding generation. Virtual sex is already upon us, holographic sex is around the corner, new devices appear to trigger new responses, and new substances constantly pour forth to fuel the engine and get more miles to the gallon. One day, humans may have the option of living in a state of perpetual orgasm, with only enough down time to ingest whatever it is you'll need to keep the good times rolling. The drive to pleasure drives on, and it does so, yes, *regardless*—because it has no capacity to "regard."

But humans do have that capacity, and using it seems to be a necessity for you. Nonetheless, whatever you look at *regardfully* has to appear to you through two filters: the filter of your human nature, and the filter of the culture you live in. What people like to call "the survival instinct," for instance, seems widely taken to be a widely shared, inherent part of human nature. It isn't universal among humans, but then I can't say I can think of any attribute that is. Lots of people give up in the face of long odds, are unwilling to soldier on, long for death, and frequently kill themselves rather than choose the path of survival. All the same, the survival instinct is common enough to have given rise to cultural constructs designed to promote survival.

I'd like to think that laws against murder grew from some kind of enlightenment, but I doubt that's the case. I suspect the law was purely practical. If there's a law that says you're not allowed to kill me, my chances of surviving go up. A law against my killing myself may seem odd; you wouldn't think my offing myself would affect *your* chances of survival one way or the other. But look at it this way: Any law that legislates the value of life serves to strengthen the cultural perception of life's value, even of life's culturally imagined "sanctity," and raises the bar when it comes to doing away with any human life—yours *or* mine, by you or by me.

I've heard that among some Indians (of the feathered variety), both killing and being killed were, under some circumstances, thought to provide added assurance of survival in a culturally-imagined afterlife. I know that among other Indians (of the red-dot variety), jumping alive into their late husbands' funeral pyres served much the same function—as did, among yet other Indians (of the high-mountain-grown variety), being a living, virginal sacrifice. The cultures that intruded upon, and then took over, these Indian societies didn't think such practices were a good idea. No matter what the cultural excuse was, you couldn't have people treating terrestrial life with such disregard, because the next thing you know, those people might treat *our* lives the same way. So in came laws against killing of all kinds. Well, almost all kinds. It was all right to kill a killer.

Domination, and its invitation to violence, is a major component of sex—more for the male, perhaps, but it's certainly not absent in the female of the species, any more than the urge to *be* dominated is absent in the male. Penetration of another body, even a penetration that is both permitted—nay, craved—and supposedly loving, contains overtones of violence. So, too, does the urge to take in, to ingest, the body of another through whatever orifice. "Honey [sic], did I ever tell you you're so adorable I could just eat you alive?"—as the female praying mantis said to her mate, right after sex and just before having his head for lunch.

Can it be true that being brought to near-death by strangulation or suffocation can enhance the euphoria of orgasm? It's certainly seems true that bondage and "discipline" and "torture" rev a lot of engines. They rev the sexual engine even when they're not in quotes, when they're the real thing. It's said that rape isn't about sex but about domination, but while I understand the distinction, it seems rather a fine one. No woman—or man, for that matter—was ever raped by a limp penis, so at least *something* sexual was going on. Sadism and masochism seem oblivious to gender, judging from the opportunities I see offered on the Internet. And whatever pleasure it is you want, if you want it badly enough, you'll go to any lengths to get it. So let there be more laws, laws against reckless driving! We must have rules of the road! We'll decide, thank you very much, where, how and with whom you can have your orgasms.

Such wishful thinking! Pile all the weight of your cultural constructions upon that urge, that drive, and still it will sprout through the cracks, like those tender, invincible sprouts of greenery that make their way through the concrete floors and walls of your cities. King Canute knew it when he sat in his thrown on the beach, letting the tide rise around him, showing his sycophantic courtiers the hollowness of their claim that he was such a mighty sovereign that he could even hold back the sea. He wasn't there to give a sex-ed lecture, but he might as well have been. The moon, that metaphor of desire, will turn, and the tides will rise. Orgasm will out. That's what it does. And the moon doesn't give a hoot what you think about the matter.

History suggests—no, that's a bad way to start this paragraph. I haven't studied history since high-school years, so what do I know? What I should have said, at the risk of repeating myself, is that after a life of random reading, a good deal of aimless traveling about, and the casual observation of an average person, it strikes me as a bad idea to invent societal constructions for humans that fly in the face of human nature. If you were an architect designing a building, wouldn't you do a better job by working with the force of gravity rather than by denying it? If you were an engineer out to dam a mighty river, wouldn't you be more likely to succeed if you took into consideration where the water would have to go after you were done?

From the look of it, the architects and engineers of human societies don't seem to think so. One the one hand, they take up the tools of force and oppression to get what they want, ignoring that it's human nature for everyone else to want to get what they want as well. *Viva la revolución!* On the other hand, they come up with ideals of behavior that are contrary to human nature and, inevitably, beyond human reach. They try to build buildings from the roof down. "We must rise above human nature!" they exclaim. That's like exhorting me to pull myself up by my own bootstraps—a noble exhortation, but don't try it if you have a bad back.

When it comes to sex, which is what we're supposed to be talking about here, and we are, because power and domination are sexy things for rulers, architects and engineers, as well as for bed mates, I have to wonder how stable, how long-lasting, any societal construction can be that relies, even in part, on celibacy and chastity to hold it up. Should anyone really be surprised that trying to dam the river of sexuality, without allowing for where the water has to go, leads to inevitable and unpredictable floods? Legislation against homosexuality strike me as a good example of humans trying to outlaw being human. The capacity to prefer sex with one's own gender is part of the human capacity, as is the need to alter one's gender in order to be at ease in one's body. Prostitution? Pornography? Pedophilia? Those "P" words are all Pejorative, all Put-downs of, whether you like it or not, components of human capacity, of what it means to be a human being. Words can't change anything. You can't stop the wind with a butterfly net—not even with one woven out of barbed wire.

There are no nice words for prostitution, pornography and pedophilia, because no one wants to be the first to invent them, to stand up in public and acknowledge there's a flip side to the pejorative. But human nature is nothing but flip sides, and not just two, like a coin. There are more flip sides to human nature than there are human beings, because each person is made up of an uncountable number of them.

So what's "right" with trading bodily pleasures for money? Mutual pleasure, that's what. One party gets the pleasure of body contact, and the other gets the pleasure of being a bit richer. If both parties leave the deal satisfied, the only "wrong" is in the sightless eyes of those blind to human nature. Take me as a case in point. There are—and bless the diversity of humankind!—young women who have a taste for a prune with a little worm hanging out of its skin, but they aren't legion, and finding them is time consuming, and time is something I haven't much of. Money helps. There's one such young woman, of whom I'm genuinely fond, whom I've helped buy her first house. She is kind and sensitive and loving. She is hard-working, honest and true. From my knowledge of her, carnal and otherwise, she merits not one pejorative word.

And what can be "right" with pornography? I'm a good one to ask about that, too; I thrive on it. My female companion of the last paragraph is often not available, and without the access technology gives me to my fantasies, I'd be a sexually lost soul most of the time. But in the good ol' privacy of my own home, I can open the good ol' plain, brown wrapper—not that I care the slightest what the mailperson thinks of what she delivers—I can pour myself a drink, light a cigarette, lay back and go for it. Relieved, I can hear the sounds of the world without sexual static. At least until the day after tomorrow.

And pedophilia? Can there be anything "right" about *that*? Here I only have second-hand knowledge, though I do know Rosario first-hand. She is 24, originally from El Salvador, and about to start her first job—as a graphic designer in a large firm—after graduating from college. I know her "father," Fred, too, but only slightly. He has retired from a career with the United Nations and lives in a neighboring village. Fred legally adopted Rosario and brought her to this country when she was 14. She often comes to visit Fred, these days with a nice, though rather yuppyish, young man she hopes to marry. She and Fred adore one another.

So how do I know there's more here than meets the eye? Because I happen to have a friend, originally a peace-corps volunteer, who was assigned to Rosario's village in El Salvador and never left. He knew Rosario and her father-to-be in the days when they first met. He not only knew Fred, but was instrumental in helping him avoid a jail term in El Salvador—something you wouldn't wish on your worst enemy, no matter what you thought of his morals. I have to qualify that: *Most* people I know wouldn't wish anyone such a fate. Fred's near miss with hell occurred when his real relationship with Rosario came to light, thanks to an evangelical missionary who stumbled on the truth of the matter. The missionary, evidently, wasn't content to think of Fred going to hell only in an afterlife. I wonder where Rosario would be now without Fred's "deviant" urges.

Another friend, Terry, whom I do know well, has another story. He's in his 50s now and also lives nearby. Terry grew up in such a dysfunctional family, to hear him tell it, that it didn't even deserve the name. He was a bright, creative kid, and he's told me that the only way he made it to the age of 15 was thanks to books and a rich fantasy life. While he was in secondary school, his English teacher singled him out for the kind of "special attention" that carries a jail term even worse than Fred's might have been. Fred's urges were at least more "normal" in their hetero cravings. I'm told that homosexual pedophiles don't fare well in the slammer.

At 15, now in high school, Terry ran away from home and effectively disappeared off the face of the earth. In fact, he secretly moved in with his former English teacher, who tutored him and introduced him to concerts, operas, ballets, plays—and travel. For the next five years the two of them lived as lovers. At 20, Terry knew in his bones that it was time for a change, time to move out into the world. He had weathered his perilous caterpillar phase, found a safe place to weave his cocoon, and now was ready to fly. His lover was wise enough, and brave enough, and *loved* Terry enough, to encourage him to take wing. Now *there's* stuff for writers to work with! Homo hearts and hetero hearts are remarkably alike in the way they pump and throb and flutter—and break.

Terry went. He went into the theater. He's still an active producer and has several enviable successes to his credit. Over the years, he and his English teacher lost touch. Terry thinks his mentor/lover may have died of AIDS. He keeps a picture by his bedside of the two of them together in front of the doors of La Scala in Milan. Terry looks impish, elfin. Beside the older man is a poster advertising *La Bohème*.

Am I promoting the pejorative Ps? No. I tell you these stories the way I might point out certain species of *flora* in the rain forest. "But *that* type's not allowed to grow here!" you protest. "The sign back there said so!" Yes, it did, but the rain forest readeth not. "We must protect children from abuse!" you insist. Now that's a good idea, let's do that. Human nature certainly has the capacity to abuse—to abuse one another regardless of age and gender, to abuse kindness itself. No, I'm not promoting abuse. In fact, I'm not "promoting" anything. This is a love letter, remember? Find your own way through the rain forest. It's a strange, exotically beautiful place, and it's dangerous, too. There are plants that will cure your wounds, but kill you to eat. Take my love with you as you explore. With that love comes a word of caring caution: Beware of throwing out the baby with the bathwater. (What on earth is a baby in a bathtub doing in the rain forest, you wonder? I told you it was an exotic place!) Or sadder still would be for you to dump (into the lush foliage around you) not only baby and water, but the whole tub as well. Beneath the suds in that bath lie glorious toys.

I'm feeling metaphorically reckless this morning. I now seem to have sex and violence not only in a rain forest, but huddled together under one umbrella. They're going to have to huddle tighter still, because here comes a third party for shelter, and that party, providing you didn't go and throw out that whole tub, is bearing an armful of the toys I mentioned. I think, or intuit, or maybe only imagine, that along with sex and violence travels creativity.

I find a lot of evidence that that's so, even if the evidence is no more than circumstantial. Let's start with sex and the *outcomes* of creativity, rather than the creative urge itself. For me, the most direct convergence is sex with music. I know *I* like sex with music. Just what it does to me, I don't know, but I know music does something, because different kinds make me feel different ways. Even before I saw whatever that movie was, Ravel's *Bolero* turned me on. I find it great foreplay music, but I don't recommend it for premature ejaculators. There's an ABBA song, "I'm all out of love," that for some reason does it for me. The great opera arias, those sweet gumdrops in what is for me an otherwise stodgy pudding, do it. You'd think Tchaikovsky and Rachmaninoff might do it, but they don't; they're all right for background at dinner, but give me Brahms in bed. Mellow jazz works fine. I can neither keep up with, nor keep it up with, rock. I can't imagine making love to rap. Voices? Ella Fitzgerald and Sarah Vaughan, yes. Eartha Kitt, yes, yes. Nina Simone, yes, yes, yes.

What is romance without low lights and music? Certain kinds of music, of course. I think the reason they pipe that sterile stuff into elevators and shopping malls is that they don't want you to have sex in elevators and shopping malls.

For me, dance comes next. Dancing with someone is a sexy thing to do, quite apart from the music you're dancing to. I've heard the reason that the waltz took the world by storm was that it was the first socially-sanctioned dance where you got to lay your hands on more than a hand. In our enlightened times, never mind the hands; you can dance like you're joined at the navel—or below—and of course that's sexy!

Even watching dance can be arousing for me. Classical ballet is a sort of reverse aphrodisiac. Its staginess and formality turn me off, while the ever-present implications of what you didn't see happening to the peasant girls at the fair, the nymphs in the woods, turns me on. I find modern, jazz-type ballet highly erotic. Fred and Ginger? You bet. I think it's their synchronization. You just know that after the tux and white tulle come off, any duo that can dance like that are going to have perfectly synchronized orgasms. Caribbean and Latino dancing are my favorites to watch. It's ALL about sex.

How art, apart from the intentionally erotic, feeds into my sexual feelings is a magical mystery, but it does. The nude figure is, naturally, apt to be suggestive, but I seldom find it arousing for what it is as a whole. Certain lines, though, especially lines of charcoal in what may be no more than the sketch of a figure, cut right to the chase. There is the caressing sweep of the contour. There's the softness of the stroke. There are varying pressures on the body you can feel as the line thickens and thins. The less I think about why it happens, the more it does.

Even if I wanted to think about my sexual responses to abstract art, I wouldn't know how. Yet, it's in front of some abstract canvases that I've felt the strongest arousal. Though I've walked—or, more often, been dragged—through a lot of museums in my time, I'm an art ignoramus. I remember few of the names of artists whose works I've seen, and I can recall almost none of the works themselves. I have next to no idea about "schools" and techniques and such. For instance, here I am, tossing around the term "abstract," when maybe what I should be tossing around is "non-representational." What I mean, anyway, are pictures where you can't see anything you can name. There's just "stuff."

My art ignorance often leaves me feeling stupid, but it could be, as far as our conversation here goes, that my ignorance is a good thing. Being incapable of *analyzing* art, all I can do is respond spontaneously. What was it about some abstract paintings I've seen that aroused me? I doubt that any number of years on a psychiatrist's couch would answer that question. I can mumble about size (domination?), or ominous feelings of threat (violence?), or sudden breaks in the textures and layers of the surface (penetration?), or sudden bursts of color amidst darkness (rosy pink amidst the pubes?), or about any amount of such nonsense. But let's leave it at this: Standing before something I couldn't understand in any way I'd learned to understand anything else, I had a sexual reaction.

Sculpture? I've met up with several sculptures I desperately wanted to caress. In fact, I'll admit I've wanted to do more than caress them. I've longed to, well, *ride* them. Imagine what those poor guards, who have to stand around all day, nicely dressed and with nothing to do, would have done if I'd given in to my fantasies, right then and there! (Come to think of it, I might have been doing one of those guards a kindness. What exciting events can he usually have to relate when his wife asks him, "How was your day, dear?" Or perhaps he asks his wife that, instead, and let's hope her job isn't handling the book returns in the public library.)

Then there's architecture. Having a sexual response to a building may be stretching the point, but I find the Guggenheim Museum in New York provocative. A soft, plushy model of it, about the size of a human being, might make an interesting sex toy, but no doubt I'll be long gone before such a thing turns up in the museum's gift shop. I remember the Gaudí buildings in Barcelona striking me as dripping with sexual innuendos. His famous Sacred Family cathedral, particularly, caught my attention with its mixture of the sensual, almost carnal, and the holy. Of course I have to remind myself that I was in Barcelona well over half a century ago at a time when just about everything I saw seemed to have something to do with sex.

Violence in the arts seems more obvious than sexuality. Music produces violence in volume and dissonance. To me, the tango is a dance of great implicit violence. Art, from cave drawings onward, has thrived on depictions of killings of all kinds. The Christian iconography is so violent that it's a wonder red paint didn't become a scarcity—all those heads on platters, martyrs coming to bad ends, and, of course, the endless crucifixions. Abstract (or whatever) art is full of head-on collisions of forms and lines. Like music, its colors can clash with dissonance or rise to the volume of a scream. Sculptural forms can poke and thrust, pierce, and seem to slash the air. And while I can't think of a particular "violent" building, the jagged environments of skyscrapers are certainly aggressive-looking and cast their long shadows over human behavior of the most downright violent sort.

(I know, skyscrapers are supposed to represent penises of some kind, but, hey, how tall does a plain old building, that's only a building, have to get before it becomes a penis? And why aren't *long* buildings ever called penises? My penis never went straight up in the air like a skyscraper, not even in my youth, not even lying on my back. I think the skyscraper-penis comparison is a fine example of how the human mind works. In comes neutral visual information, up and around your skull it goes, like it's doing a loop-the-loop on a roller coaster, and lo and behold! What you think you see is what you'd like to see, because what you'd like to see confirms what you'd like to believe. Most men I've met would much rather see their penises as a skyscraper in Manhattan than as a four-story tenement in the Bronx. It's truly a nifty illusion factory, that thing up there on our shoulders.)

Enough about penises and about my reactions to the outcomes of the creative urge. I'd like to speculate about the nature of the urge itself, and whether sex and violence may play a part in egging it on. Or is it the other way around? Just who is it who's egging on whom under that umbrella in the rain forest?

I've been talking about "the arts" so far and giving "business" short shrift. Maybe that's because it's easier for me to look at a piece of art and tell you my reaction than it is for me to observe a piece of business and respond. Business is a different kettle of fish, a horse of a different color. What else can I throw in here? Business outcomes and artistic outcomes are apples and oranges, chalk and cheese! That should do it.

Business seems to be everywhere that humans come together. Is there any reason to doubt that it's business, in one way or another, that occupies the vast majority of the days and energies of the vast majority of human lives? I don't think so, and I also don't doubt that it's business that consumes the overwhelming share of human creativity. Having gone out on that limb, I suppose I should take a stab at saying what I think creativity is. Someone said that creativity was taking known components and rearranging them into new combinations that produce a new result. That works for me.

The business of business definitely fits that definition. In business, competition is the name of the game, and what else are innovative products and services and practices but new arrangements of the already known? And is there sex and violence in the marketplace? I have to laugh even writing such a rhetorical question. Look at such common phrases as "ruthless competition" and "hostile takeovers," and, on the softer, more sexual side, "mergers." But that's only surface talk. Anyone who's worked in a large corporation knows that there's plenty of sex and violence down in the everyday, nitty-gritty life of office corridors.

Where else outside of the arts can we look? How about science and academia, two other arenas which absorb a lot of human time? There's tons of creativity going on there, all right. Science may have no rival in rearranging known elements into new structures. What are all those academic researchers in their cubbyholes doing but reformulating available information into new hypotheses about how and why history unfolded the way it did? Any violence and sex around in either scientific or academic circles? Does anyone ever do any "backstabbing" there? Any hanky-panky ever take place in the lab or the library? Could it be that getting head ever had anything to do with getting ahead? Of course it could, from the casting couch to the Oval Office, and everywhere in between.

I suppose the most basic act of creation among humans is the creation of a baby, and the definition of creativity I'm using certainly fits that situation—taking two existing sets of genes, rearranging them, and producing a new outcome. Is that where it all starts?

I don't know what Henry Ford said when he whisked the tarp off the prototype Model T, but it could have been, "There's my baby!" Those in the arts, too, have a way of talking about their works as their "babies." The analogy is a good one for all creative spirits, and maybe that's all it is, an analogy.

After all, there's the urge to create something. There's the coming together of urge and imagination, the "Aha!" orgasm. There's the "seminal" idea, the seed planted in the brain. There's the long period of incubation. And there's the "going into labor" of getting whatever it is out into the world.

I don't think that analogy is accidental. I think there's something else going on here besides playing with words, something else that, in fact, has nothing to do with words. It has to do with a feeling, a *need*, even, that so many creators of things—including parents—have expressed. It's the need to leave something of themselves behind when they die, be it a baby, a canvas, a discovery, a thesis, a composition or a corporation. It's the need creators seem to feel to defy death, in some way continue into subsequent generations. Even as an outsider, with no urges toward continuation in any form, I can empathize and understand what a compelling, natural, human need that could be. I can even imagine it taking precedence over all the other speculative possibilities about what the origins of the creative urge may be.

What *is* going on under that umbrella in the rain forest? What is the umbrella anyway, and which of the three candidates beneath it—sex, violence and creativity—is holding it up? I'd say its creativity that has the firmest grip on the handle, but it may not be; it's become blurry out there in the rain. As for what the umbrella is, that's simple. It's The Flow that is perpetually mating and exploding into new combinations. It's what happens, that's all—has forever and forever will. All of human creativity is only a microscopic expression, the most miniscule expression imaginable, of the great array of constant creation that's going on out there. But tiny though it is, in it the vastness of The Flow is revealed.

Good Heavens!

I was lying in my hammock by the pond the other day, somewhere between a snooze and awake, in a state of mind I've come to like more and more. I call it going doggish. It's the way I imagine a dog feels lying on a familiar carpet, with familiar humans around, talking and laughing, coming and going in familiar ways, giving off familiar smells. There's no danger that requires alertness. No one's calling me to come. No one's throwing a stick for me to go fetch. I'm not hungry or thirsty. My body functions are quiet. (And how rare that's getting for me these days!) I just *am*.

I was sort of in neutral. If I'd been in a state to think about it, I'd have known that all around me everything was speeding along at its usual pace, and that inside me, too, constant changes were going on as busy cells went about doing both the mischief and repair that cells do. But I wasn't in a thinking state at all. The occasional thought that bubbled up from somewhere, out of habit, I suppose, burst and disappeared without a trace.

Is this doggish space the space people try to get to through chanting and meditation? For me, the very act of *trying* to go doggish will send me in the opposite direction, send me squirrelish—even *trying* to let doggishness just happen all by itself.

I doubt that drugs can make you doggish, though I've known people who claim they can. Getting stoned, either on the sly or by a doctor's prescription, seems to me to be interrupting some body-mind activities or inducing others. That sort of intentional intervention isn't part of what I mean by getting doggish.

Trust me: If you want to improve your chances of reaching doggishness, all you need to do is get old, and that doesn't take any trying at all.

Where was I, anyway? Oh yes, lying there, doggish, in my hammock.

There was a backdrop in front of my slightly open eyes, indistinct and abstract. I wasn't looking at it exactly, because looking at something brings it into focus and engages the brain in the effort to make out what it is. A connection springs up between the outside of you and the inside, and I didn't feel connected to anything. I was aware, but nothing more, aware of a web of fuzzy lines that bled off here and there into blue. If I'd hit the focus button and started looking, my eyes would have begun darting around in my head, and I'd have seen the wisps of my eyelashes entwined with the branches of the tree that was holding up my hammock at my feet, and beyond the branches, the sky.

But I didn't hit the focus button. In fact, I was so deeply doggish that I didn't even think about doing so. What was before my eyes had no foreground or background, no names, no logic. It had no relation to me, and I had none to it. At some point, no thanks to any effort of mine, the web of lines disintegrated altogether and all there was was blue. *I* was blue. Blue was *me*—at least as much as I was anything right then.

Doggishness comes and goes as it will. Out of that all-blue everything, there emerged a visualization, an image, an image in focus, the image of a memory. It came from a trip I'd taken to Kansas City years ago, so many years ago that I can't even swear for sure that it was Kansas City, but I think it was. I'm standing on the observation deck of a small building at a small airport out in the countryside, and even from what can't be more than three storeys up, I can see the sky touching the flat horizon all around me. I am in the exact center of a circle beneath a bright, blue bowl.

With that image, out of doggishness I came, as though someone had thrown a stick and said "Go fetch!" only in this case the stick was a thought. I'm not in Kansas City anymore. I'm in the cortex of my brain, and I'm looking around at the inside of my blue skull. And then more thoughts come tumbling in willy-nilly, and I'm back, wide-awake, in my hammock by the pond, thinking. I'm thinking about you, as I so often do. What is it about you that makes the simplicity of living and dying so complicated, such a trial?

That's a hefty question, isn't it? It's not only ponderous but also crackles with emotional electricity. I want to talk to you about it, though, perhaps more than about anything else. In doing so, I'm going to try to tread gingerly, with kindness and compassion, empathy and understanding. To do so, I have to speak from my *otherness* from you, but I'll try not to leave my human heart behind.

I sometimes wonder if there's something about the curvature of the human skull itself that bends ideas and sends them back down upon you. I see you as if you're inside a great cathedral—St. Peter's in Rome, perhaps, or St. Paul's in

London—shooting arrows of ideas at the distant, domed ceiling. No matter how high the arrows fly, down they have to come again, hitting someone in the eye. Your urge to archery is a marvel. Any idea you can find a way to notch to your bowstring is fair game.

Your philosophers, for instance, are endlessly resourceful. Up go their latest theories with a great *thwang!* Some among the watching crowd applaud those arrows in their flight, but then down the arrows come again, sharp ends first. The injured, naturally enough, want revenge. The scientists among you are, of course, yeomen bowmen, but lately they've taken to firing lethal rockets instead of arrows. Carried away by their boundless enthusiasm, scientists frequently miss or mistake their targets. Their rocketing ideas hit all sorts of things, philosophers included. Scientific theories soar for a while, but sooner or later they have to follow the curvature of the human skull, too, and down they come.

One of the current scientific ideas in flight seems to be that space, itself, is curved just like the skull. I wonder if that's only a coincidence. I'd be the last to know, math and science, as I've said, having been my downfall in school. All the same, there are things that I know from my strange position among you, and one of them is that space is not "curved," any more than it's shaped like an ampersand or an exclamation mark. There's nothing either curved or straight out there unless a human is looking. It's like that old, self-contradictory nonsense about whether the falling tree makes a sound if there's no one there to hear it. Space is only curved if a curved mind is thinking about it. Curved space is a wonderfully creative vision, and one, it seems, that has proved a big help in making the workings of the universe able to be argued about among minds that live in their own curved spaces. I'd like to be around to hear what the next, unexpected, astonishing, shape-of-space arrow will be that goes flying up there before it, too, comes down.

It's a form of gravity that brings all these arrows back to earth, but not the gravity you're used to thinking about. Human nature has its own kind of gravity built in, and like the other kind of gravity that has to do with physics, human nature's gravity won't be denied. You are what you are, and you'll never be something else. Oh yes, you'll go on endlessly surprising yourselves with new discoveries about what you are, how you're put together and what you can do. Well, not "endlessly," but as long as you're around. But for as long as that may be, you'll never become anything other than what you are, anything that didn't grow out of the essence of being human in the first place. You'll never overcome that essential gravity of human nature.

"Hold on a minute!" you say. "We've come a long way, baby, a long, long way from that whatever-it-was that crawled out of that soupy lagoon! Who knows where we'll end up?"

True, true. That whatever-it-was didn't look much like today's venture capitalist in an Armani suit, but it already had the capacity, even as it made its way up onto dry land, to venture capital and to sprout the arms and legs that Mister Armani's suit would need. As to where you'll end up, yes, who's to say? Certainly not me. It would seem that you're well on the way to altering what you are today into something different. If news stories are getting it right, you can already alter yourselves genetically, and it seems a certainty that soon you'll be able to photocopy yourselves at will, creating warehouses of replaceable parts. You're on the threshold of becoming "bionic," whatever that really means and whatever it may lead to after that.

Being human is an ongoing capacity, not a fixed point, that's for sure. But even an ongoing capacity in constant transformation cannot go beyond what it's capable of doing, can it? There is stuff that's always bound to be beyond your reach, even though the gravity of human nature will always make you refuse to believe it. That's not a bad thing. It may even be a good thing. Whichever it is, your glorious denial of the truth of the matter, the truth that you'll never be able to understand everything, is one of your characteristics I cherish most. I love its optimism, its panache, its quality of derring-do. What's more, your sense of adventure guarantees that, as a species, you'll always be on the move, always out there breaking new ground on the way to staking out new mirages.

There's a problem, though. What's a creature, that thinks it can know everything, supposed to do with the things it doesn't know? If everything has to be named, understood and categorized, where are the cubbyholes for the unknown? The idea of gods provided nifty cubbyholes for a while. These usually more-or-less humanoid creations served to take up the slack in what humans didn't understand and couldn't control. Think for a minute what a rich array of cultural treasures has sprung out of this ancient need to find places to put things. What legends and literature! What art and artifacts! What buildings and monuments! What rituals! What music! It doesn't matter that it's all a fabric of ingenious inventions. Would any of you have it any other way? Certainly not travel agents, a slew of whom I can see out there emphatically shaking there heads.

There are so many marvelous maps of "The Beyond." That it's *beyond* hasn't daunted the cartographers one single bit. Like every other idea, the very concept of "beyond" hit the domed ceiling of the skull and came back down. Not even it could pierce the vault and fly free, even though the names it acquired suggested that was what it was supposed to do, and, in some cases, went so far as to suggest that's what it had actually gone and done. Some of the tags I can think of that have been attached to The Beyond include the ineffable, the sublime, the numinous, the divine, Nirvana and Heaven, not to mention "that which passeth human understanding." That last one would seem to say it all, but it, too, is subject to human gravity and has demanded justification, explanation, a structure of logic of some kind. How human of you—and how irresistibly seductive of you—to establish something that is, in your own words, unknowable . . . and then to insist on describing it!

The many realms of The Beyond have a perplexing assortment of names. In my case, I grew up in a family that was loosely Protestant—an historical name rooted in bitter conflict over how to know the unknowable. My parents were content with the Christmas and Easter rituals and would probably have left church-going at that, except for some social obligation they felt toward raising their only child in a socially acceptable fashion. This means that we did go to church from time to time of a Sunday, but only if my parents didn't have a more compelling offer on the table—like a round of golf or the need to sleep off the revelry of Saturday night. My father had been raised Baptist, but he jumped ship when he married and happily boarded my mother's sleek, Episcopalian yacht. The crew in her nation's navy had nattier uniforms, the food and drink were more varied and plentiful, and he found the company of her fellow passengers more entertaining than his. What's more, unlike life aboard his original, sturdy, working vessel, the passengers on the St. Bede weren't expected to scrub the decks or heave on the lines.

Dad's family didn't approve of his changing ships like that. They considered him a soul in danger aboard an unseaworthy craft. They worried, particularly, about me and prayed constantly not only for my safe passage, but for my return to their crew. I hardly knew my father's family. My memories of the few times we got together, usually for a brief appearance at a wedding or a funeral, have blurred into one polite standoff, during which each side of the family pretends to enjoy the food on the other's table. Dad's family ate much more than Mom's. They really chowed down on basics like fried chicken and green-Jello-and-marshmallow salads. They tended to be heavy people. We picked at smoked salmon, sipped white wine, and were skinny.

My parents never bad-mouthed Dad's family for their habits or beliefs. I can't recall them ever bad-mouthing anyone from any nation of The Beyond.

Coexistence with their Jewish friends was easy. Where we lived, there were enough country clubs to go around, and whatever rituals went on at home or with the like-minded were no one else's business. It wasn't that easy with the Roman Catholics we knew. The separation of space and custom was less defined. The Jews, you could say, had their own destination resort which we never visited, just as they never visited ours. For some reason, on the other hand, the Catholics and the Protestants had to try to share the same physical and social spaces. It seemed to work out most of the time, the citizens of the two nations minding their manners with one another and treating one another with at least a superficial, mutual respect. Back when I was growing up, it was mainly issues of intermarriage and how to raise the children that brought the deep fault lines to the surface. When that happened, things could turn nasty, but at least we shared a space where it was agreed you had to check your weapons at the door. My peculiar vantage point among you lets me stand back and watch these goings-on without getting caught up in traditional allegiances or historical feuds. To me, as I look at the immeasurably bountiful cornucopia of the night sky, such bones of contention don't seem nourishment worth the effort to chew on.

I did chew a bit in college, though. I couldn't avoid the heated philosophical and religious discussions that swirled around me, and I wouldn't have wanted to evade them even if I could have. I didn't learn a whole lot about what I was meant to be learning with my parents' money, but I learned volumes and volumes of extra-curricular material from my group of close friends who knew, with the greatest certainty, that their parents and forbears had got everything wrong, that there was no one in charge who could be trusted, and that once they were sprung from the hard labor of their academic prison, they were going to put things right. Some of these friends wrote impassioned polemics that got themselves labeled—to their delight—subversive. They marched in the streets whenever they could find a banner of dissent from The Establishment to raise above their heads.

Passion! It was all about passion. It's hard for me to date when my uncertain confusions about you turned into a love affair, but I think it was back in those college days when passion sizzled in the air around me. I felt out of it, on the sidelines, but passion is a fierce contagion, and I remember longing to get infected.

Almost all of my close college friends vanished soon after we graduated. The arrows of their ideas didn't have much lift, and those once-upon-a-time revolutionaries melted effortlessly into that world they had seen as ill-formed, unjust, and ripe for remaking. I have no idea what became of them. Only with two of those friends did our friendship survive long enough for their names to make it through several dog-eared address books, and only one of the two has stayed alive to make it into my current, antiseptic list of e-mail contacts. The one who died, several years ago but at ripe age, I miss very much.

Our lives were nothing alike. He was a musician, given to lavish excess, and unconventionally brilliant in both his craft and his talent for survival. He never made it big, but he made everything he touched bigger than life. For him, each day was a lifetime of its own, to be lived to the fullest. There was no question of keeping up with his pace, but even tagging along behind brought me as close to human passion as I've ever come. "Religion"? The word wasn't even the tiniest of blips on his radar screen During our college days, when he was already playing a mean guitar and sax, his only contribution to our late-night, boozy, philosophical and religious discussions was the background music, the rhythms and progressions of his passion.

My other college friend, who's still alive, lives far away with his enormous family. We've been managing to get together every couple of years, but now it's become as hard for him to travel as it is for me. We both know we may have seen the last of each other. We've agreed that neither of us has to try to make the trek to the other's funeral. He is a quiet and deeply religious man—not a zealot, or we wouldn't have stayed friends all these years. His religious affiliation has a name, but I won't name it because I don't want you to put him in a pigeonhole. Knowing him as well as I do, I feel safe in saying that the core of his religious belief is to do with human relationships. For him, each encounter with another human being is a kind of religious experience—whether it's with a stranger asking him for directions, or a family member in need of advice or comfort. His passion is all the louder for making so little noise. I crave his company, and thank heavens for the Internet.

It was a long time before I met, let alone got to know, a true Evangelical, a Mormon, or a Jehovah's Witness. When I did, passion crackled around me once again. I have yet to meet a Seventh Day Adventist, but in the unlikely event that I do, I'm sure I'll feel that same, electric "rush." It was longer still, not until my years of travel, before the passion of Buddhism, Hinduism or Islam zapped me. What awesome diversity there is in the human spirit's quest to know the unknowable! When I heard about the Jones group, who went their way on poisoned Kool-Aid, and the group which chased after the comet in their Nikes, and the Branch Dividians, whom we watched on television go up in flames, I had to bite my tongue among even my dearest friends. My coming to passion's defense would only have ended in all of us floundering around in the sticky mud of words.

We're already in that mud bath here, you and I, so we might as well press on and get as muddy as we can. It will all wash off in the end.

When, from my outsider's perspective, I look at all that you lump together as "religion," I feel I'm looking at stunning cityscape at night. I see edifices of almost every conceivable design, some even seeming to defy humdrum gravity, all brightly lit, fueled by human passion. There that city lies, taking up the whole horizon, a breathtaking sight, the sort of special-effects thing sci-fi movie people come up with, only more so. It's one big WOW! In the movies, such cityscapes exist only on other planets, but here it is, right here on Earth, and, believe me, there's nothing like it anywhere "out there."

And to think that this mind-boggling metropolis all sprang out of the little bone box above your neck! How could such a marvel be? Are there no limits to what you can think up?

Yes, there are limits, the same old limits there will always be. There's the invincible force of human nature's own gravity, and there's the curvature of the human skull. That's why, if we enter the thoroughfares of that glowing metropolis, we'll find the doors of the buildings locked against intruders with armed guards posted in the lobbies, riot police standing watch at the intersections, and in the dark alleys, rival gangs roaming the night, slaughtering one another without so much as a second thought. If we dared get close to these assassins, we'd see they don't look like the dispossessed in the ordinary cities we live in. They're extremely well dressed. Their knives are beautifully crafted. Their firearms are new and sleek, the latest models. It would be foolish to try to follow these murderous bandits home, but if we did, we'd find them living, not in cardboard boxes on the sidewalks, but up in the penthouses of these monumental buildings. A little investigation would reveal that some of them paid to have their buildings built in the first place, insisting their building outshine its neighbor and be the best on the block.

You may find all that urban violence upsetting, and I know you won't find comfort in my telling you it doesn't matter the way you think it does. The capacity for violence is an inevitable . . . inseparable . . . integral . . . essential . . . *necessary* part of passion, and passion is what brought that fantasy skyline up out of the ground to begin with. Enough of fantasy, though. Look around you. What is it *you* care most about? Go ahead, look for it. Look *at* it. Touch it. Feel it. Embrace it. It's there, in what you hold dearest, that you'll find your passion, and along with it, your own capacity for violence.

For something to matter to you, you have to have feelings for it. In the ordinary sense of the word, it matters plenty to you, I know, if someone you love is killed by a stray bullet in a bank-robbery shootout. That matters deeply and painfully—just as it mattered to me when the wife I adored was killed in the Colorado mountains. It mattered to me, too, when I was assaulted and robbed that night in Pernambuco. I'm not playing games with you, believe me, when I tell you it doesn't matter in The Great Scheme of Things, in what you might call the "cosmic" sense, in what I've been calling The Flow. That's because feelings don't exist there. They exist only here, among you, among *us*.

As usual, we've run aground on the reef of words—in this case, the verb "to matter." It's hard enough for you to agree among yourselves what matters. What matters to you may be of no significance to your neighbor and vice versa. That state of affairs can put you and your neighbor at loggerheads. It can even lead you to violence out of your passion for what matters to *you*. For you, your neighbor and, possibly, the police, that violence may seem a serious outcome, but from where I stand, at least from where *part* of me stands, whether you kill you neighbor or your neighbor kills you—over the noise his lawnmower makes at 6 in the morning or over your belief in God—couldn't "matter" less. The Flow goes on regardless.

Stars, as scientists like to put it, are born and die as well. Of course they do neither, but scientists are hobbled by words just like the rest of us. Stars take shape from what is and always has been, and they break apart into what is and always has been. Their comings and goings don't matter, either, even though those same scientists are preoccupied with matters of matter and anti-matter. Here's a question for you: If a star in space explodes into a supernova, does it make a noise if there's no one there to hear it? That question is easier than the old one about the tree falling in the forest. When was the last time anyone heard a supernova explode? Can anyone tell me if the sound is louder or softer than that of a falling tree?

Enough games. It's a matter of perspective, isn't it? While we're on the subject of trees and forests, there's that other saying that someone who is blind to the larger picture "can't see the forest for the trees"—whether that person can hear them falling or not. When a person dies, does it matter if there's no one around to grieve? When it comes to what matters or doesn't matter, perspectives play a big part in arriving at an answer.

Let's go back into our fantasy city. From the perspective of a visitor lost in those violent streets, the city is a place of mayhem and terror. But let's imagine that you and I are looking at that city from afar, from up on a hill, drinking champagne on the balcony of a restaurant—probably an overpriced restaurant for tourists like us. As we marvel at that glowing skyline, we lift our glasses in a toast to human ingenuity. We might even "be moved to tears" by the awesome beauty of the spectacle below us. If I'm acting a little strange, a little distracted, as we sit there together, over our white linen tablecloth with its romantic little candle in the middle, I beg you to forgive me. Because of the way I am, I'm not able to be fully present. Part of me sees the city as you do, but part of me is seeing it from farther off, from far, far off in the night sky. There, in the whirling galaxies and amidst the soundless explosions of supernovas, neither the mayhem nor the beauty below us matter. Nothing matters in the human sense of the word. There are no tears to be moved to, not a single tear to be shed. Not over anything.

Shall we cut to the chase? We might as well, because we already sort of did when God slipped into our conversation a while ago as one possible cause of violence between neighbors—God and the noise of an early-morning lawnmower. Besides, I imagine He's been gesturing impatiently from the wings of your mind for some time.

God poses a problem. In fact two of them. There's a problem of gender, and there's a problem of typography. Should God really be a "he"? And then, on top of the he-or-she problem, should whichever personal pronoun be capitalized? I'm not being flippant. These are not trivial concerns. The implications within these questions lie like stepping-stones across lakes of human blood. Even my raising the questions with you here is likely to have raised your blood pressure a notch or two. Raised pressure makes blood spurt all the faster, as any heretic, slammed to death on the spikes of the Iron Maiden, can tell you.

In our culture, the gender question seems to have been decided long ago. God, along with Jehovah, are to be considered male. Western religions are not alone in this of course. Allah is male, and Krishna is male. Buddha, though from the little I understand not in the same category, has a category which is his and not hers. There may be little agreement over other aspects of spirituality or religion, but it seems that most of the world's people who are followers of one belief or another have conferred the ultimate authority on a "him." Or a capital H "Him." If you happen to think things should have worked out otherwise and want to revise the situation, all I can say is "good luck!"—and you'd do well to choose carefully where you live. As it's not an issue for me, I'll go along with the druthers of the majority.

I hope you and I don't have to get hung up on typography, either. It's bad enough to be hung up on words and what they mean, without having to worry as well about how they get written. Bearing in mind that I'm not intending to imply anything at all by the way I hit these little keys on the keyboard, can we agree to accept the most commonly used forms? All I'm trying to do is enable us to get on with our conversation, and in that pursuit, I'm going to be giving God—you know, the one on the dollar bill—a big G so that we can identify, yes, capital H Him. The other look-alikes are going to get small "g"s, and while that may not seem fair to some of you, remember we're only talking about hitting the "shift" key now and then.

I imagine it's obvious I don't know much about capital R Religion. I've already told you I took a course in comparative religions in college and nearly flunked it. But academic knowledge wouldn't help here, anyway. All I'm talking about is your admirable, unquenchable urge to know the unknowable. I find it a heroic quest. For me, it all boils down to your refusing to take "no" for an answer, and that refusal continues to propel you along your way. Someone once gave me this advice: "Always aim for the moon, because, that way, you might at least end up on top of the nearest lamp post." And look what's happened! You not only aimed for the moon, you planted a flag on it! I take off my hat to you.

I feel I owe it to you, all the same, to let you know where I'm coming from as we talk about religion and such. It seems only fair, and in doing so, I'm not trying to lay upon you any version of a "truth." I'm just trying to let you know me better.

The way I've come to imagine it, back in Valley A and Valley B, when humans were swapping grunts, trading blows, and getting off with each other's women, knowing the unknowable was, most likely, already a priority. Somebody had to make sense, for instance, of The Thing No One Can Look At, the thing that brought light and heat. Then there was that thing's enemy, darkness, that kept interrupting the hunt. There were big, black, noisy apparitions that came swooping overhead and ruined prehistoric picnics and parades. What were they all about? Where did they come from and where did they go?

A top priority, I imagine, was understanding the workings of that living, dancing, alluring—but dangerous and fickle—creature that made the cave cosy in winter, cooked your meat, and provided light so you could paint pictures on the walls. It could bite you, too, if you got too close to it, and sometimes it up and vanished, just like that, leaving you in a dark and chilly lurch.

How could there not have been the urgent urge to understand these things and bring them under control, to make them friends and allies? Where would you all be today if there hadn't been such an urge? The first order of business back then must have been to give these phenomena names—grunts of special importance, grunts that merited the "shift" key—at least in tone of voice—and special marks on the cave wall, and even special emblems you could carry around with you. These mysterious marvels became transformed, at least the way I like to think of it, into The Gods of the Grunts. And that's the last time they'll get capital letters.

What were these gods supposed to look like? If they were to look like something, they had to look like something that was around for them to look like, right? *We're* the most important things around, our ancestors thought, and what's more, we're the ones deciding all this, so the most important gods must look something like us. I doubt that humility was our ancestors' strong suit, but they had to see that they weren't the *only* important things around. There were important animals and important plants, for example, so maybe some of them had better be gods as well.

Deciding on genders must have been easy. Strength and force went, naturally, to the males, because anyone could see they were "guy" things. When it came to birth, however, whether from the belly or the earth, the guys had to defer. That deep mystery was clearly "gal" stuff—and stuff to be treated with great respect. Even the strongest and most forceful male would have known that without some of that important gal stuff, he wouldn't have even been around to grunt.

Who knows how these things really worked themselves out? Not I, for sure. But however they did so, there were bound to be variations between Valley A's version and Valley B's. Now they had something big to grunt and fight about. Whose gods were the most powerful and best? Whose were the *real* gods?

As they saying goes, "The more things change, the more they stay the same." Isn't it the truth?

I need to make a detour here. That little saying which sprung so easily to my mind makes me think again of Tchaikovsky—and of his grand, romantic melodies that went from brainstorm, to feverish scribbling of ink on paper, to the cold feet of an opening-night premiere in Moscow, to concert halls around the world, to movie soundtrack, to Golden Classics that scroll down the television screen, to pop song, and into the elevator-music repertoire wherever there are elevators. The music is so direct to the heart, as instantly affecting as a lip-smacking kiss from a stranger—a kiss right on the ear. Like such a kiss, the music is *too* direct, *too* affecting. We didn't have to work hard enough to figure out the message, so the message can't be worth much. It's obvious. It's trite. We can disregard it and move on to something more intellectually challenging. The curvature of the skull has brought Tchaikovsky's beautifully fletched arrows back, blunt and harmless, to the cold, linoleum, elevator floor.

I was taught not to mix metaphors, but damn the torpedoes! "The more things change, the more they stay the same" leaps to the mind and rolls effortlessly off the tongue, slips with no friction into an awaiting ear, skips like a flat stone across the surface of the brain within, and trickles out the ear the other side. There it evaporates.

I'm proud of that sentence. Every English teacher I ever had would have flunked me.

As to what all that has to do with the price of eggs, as they say, I'm not sure, which is why I called for a detour. I think that it has to do with the human compulsion I see around me to shy away from the big and the obvious. The universe is big, and humans' place in it is, to me, obvious. Yet, the grandeur and beauty of the situation seem to make you shy away from facing it. First, you reduce the obvious grandeur and beauty of The Flow to something else that has the manageable proportions of Earth, to proportions your human minds can encompass. Then, you invest those reductions with a different grandeur and beauty of your own making. Such a complicated and unnecessary exercise! And one that obscures the obvious, which is so simple! So it was with our ancestors. They were human, too.

Yes, things change but stay the same. That's a big and obvious observation, and nowadays it, like a Tchaikovskian grand theme, is considered trite. Nonetheless, that trite observation is worth grabbing as it flies by. Scientists won't ever come up with a better in-a-nutshell description of how the universe works than saying that it's ever-changing and ever the same. But they'll go on trying.

Scientists' efforts in the early days of their profession must have given the keepers of the gods bad headaches. Mystery had to keep beating a retreat into those areas science still couldn't reach. Those areas grew smaller and smaller, leaving less and less room for a multitude of deities. Somewhere along the way, the keepers came up with a good, space-saving idea: One takes up less room than many. Let's hit the shift key, and let there be God! But a God of the Gaps, as someone put it, wasn't a satisfying god. To merit a capital letter, He had to be omnipotent, the creator of all things, including, of course, science and scientists, along with the nature, origins and outcomes of Eternity—areas that to the God-inclined were likely to lie beyond scientific meddling for a good long time to come. They were certainly right about that.

Origins and outcomes, however, were relatively small matters. There was the biggie—the Big Question, the mystery that obviously, judging from what archeologists have unearthed, perplexed the inhabitants of both Valley A and Valley B, just as it perplexes you today and will perplex you tomorrow and tomorrow and tomorrow: the scientifically unchartable, unapproachable, terrain of "the afterlife." Right from the git-go, the terrain of life after death was the province of the gods, and then it became capital G God's realm, His kingdom.

I wonder why the whole issue of an afterlife didn't go the other way. The very notion that there might be such a thing might never have occurred to anyone at all. Early human beings could have developed in such a way that they were content to see themselves as things that came and went like everything else. Being "here today and gone tomorrow" could have taken root in the human mind as the way the world worked, no questions asked. Such a view must have been the logical one. Even primitive eyes could see that every other creature that moved upon the land, swam in the waters, or flew through the air had its time and then grew still and turned into dust—or sometimes into dinner. Trees grew and fell, noisily or not, creeks dried up, and even cliffs crumbled. Who needed to know more that that?

Perhaps one day someone will pinpoint why and when the human mind took a sharp left turn from the seemingly obvious and set off, instead, in the direction of Oz. Until that day, our guesses are as good as any. My guess as to the why is this: because of the same fear of the dark that played such a large role in conjuring up the gods in the first place. As for the when, I think it happened as soon as there was a little child who didn't want to go to bed without a light left on.

Death as a long sleep, and sleep as a short death, have been the stuff of poetry, probably for as long as poetry has been around, and that's probably ever since our valley dwellers discovered even some grunts rhymed. The French brought sex into it, too, but let's not go there. The fact is, many parents still like to tell their children that Grandpa has gone to sleep forever. Children are smart. Go to sleep *forever*? Who wants to risk that? Tell me another story, Mom! Leave a light on in the hall!

When I look in the mirror these days, I see myself as an old onion. I like to think what I see is a sweet, old Vidalia onion, but that's not for me to say. The layers of the years have formed around me, but the soft center of my human infancy is still in there somewhere. Isn't that the way it is for all of us?

Tiny tots of course want to know they're going to wake up in the morning, and the layers of the years don't change anything. Grownups, at least billions of them, want to know that they're going to wake up from death—that long, long sleep—in an afterlife of some kind. As for me, I can't be sure anymore that I *will* wake up in the morning when I go to bed, and I know that if I don't, I'm not going to wake up in any afterlife, either. That knowledge brings me no fear, because I know, too, that there's nothing to be afraid of. If I could give you only one thing as I leave, it might be that—the comforting certainty there's nothing to fear in death.

Some people fear an imaginary Judgment Day. Judgment Days serve a purpose, but next Thursday's as good as any other. You could spend a moment before you go to bed looking back at what you did and didn't do and see how you feel about it. You be the judge.

A fair amount of money must have changed hands over the centuries from people wanting to talk to loved ones who have awakened "on the other side." A good deal changes hands today. The widow of a friend of mine recently spent $250 trying to make a connection, and that's an expensive long-distance phone call—especially when you have to pay up whether you get through or not. She didn't, at least not in the way she'd hoped. She's positively eager to die. Her life has turned sour in many ways, and she finds almost no joy left in living. She's a woman with great faith in her religion, and she prays regularly to God to take her so that she can rejoin her late husband, my friend, who was a gentle, considerate and loving spouse. She wants to "go to sleep" and "wake up" in his company in the afterlife, and she has no doubt that's what's going to happen when she dies. She's very open about her belief, and she's equally open about a problem that vexes her—the problem that made her engage that expensive operator. Her problem is this:

She had two unfortunate marriages that ended in bitter divorces before she lucked into her many happy years with my friend. Those two previous husbands are both dead as well, and she wonders if she's going to have to deal with them again, too, when she wakes up. Her $250 didn't bring any answers to that question.

Visions of an afterlife are wondrous things. This world would be so much less colorful and less interestingly textured without them as a backdrop. They have enabled so many of you to find a "meaning" to life here that human nature seems compelled to seek. I think these visions are marvelous, and I'm all for there being as many as you can think up. What makes me sad is seeing the gravitational force of human nature bring these particular arrows down with such collateral damage. Does there really have to be only one vision? Does it really have to dominate the others? I'd have thought the unknowable should have had as many unanswers as possible for people to choose from. Why the insistence that only one vision be right and all the others wrong?

Why? Because. Because that's how you're made. All the same, it's not how things are.

Out there in The Flow, there's no such thing as right and wrong. Events occur. One thing leads to another, setting off consequences of all kinds all over the place. None of these consequences are either good or bad. They have no "meaning." They don't "matter." The Flow simply goes on doing its thing, as it always has and always will. Humans have happened as part of its "thing." In Flow terms, we won't be around long. Whatever you think up while you're here makes no lasting difference whatsoever. In Flow terms, whether you're kind or cruel to one another in your passing affects nothing. How you act will neither win you bonus points nor earn you demerits in any final exam. It won't advance or delay you on your pilgrimage to an imagined afterlife.

"But what of the prophets?" you ask. Are their words meaningless? Worse, were they all con men, threatening punishments and promising rewards where there were none to be had? Well, it's true they were *men* for the most part, in cultures that were run by men, and that in itself might make you wonder a little. There are venerated women, to be sure, but they seem to occupy a lower place in the pecking order of the prophets. Even Mother Earth and Mother Nature, when exalted and worshipped, seem more diffuse, less authoritarian, than the male figures who have shaped our lives and handed down rules of behavior.

I see anthropologists urgently raising their hands, vying for floor time. I defer. Yes, there may be a society, a culture somewhere, where God in *Her* glory reigns supreme. My guess is that even there, deciding how Her day-to-day affairs are to be ordered is likely to be the province of men, who get to determine what Her wishes are and what happens to you if you obey those wishes or don't. If my guess is wrong, I stand corrected, but wherever that society may be, it's far out of the mainstream and exists as an object of curiosity and study.

From my perspective, though, the point is not so much that the prophets were either male or female as that they were human. Some cultures have upped the ante on prophets by deciding they were human only for a while, that they dropped into human affairs from a divine ether, and that after a series of adventures and misadventures, they returned to the unknowable from where they came. Believe it, by all means, if you want, but the good news for some and the bad news for others is that these prophets were born as human as you are and died the same. You may need to think otherwise, and being the products of their human cultures, even some of the prophets may have thought otherwise, but that's how it is. The Flow continues, mindless of their comings and goings.

What I think the prophets did was to bring a small, fragile part of human nature to the fore, to make it stand out against the clamor and mayhem of the streets of the city we've imagined out there on the nighttime skyline. Those streets are dizzying, blinding with their flashing neon come-ons, but the prophets were able to raise signs that outshone the rest—signs that read "acceptance," "tolerance," "self-sacrifice," and shining brightest of all, "compassion." The prophets' greatest gift to you was to keep those signs bright above their doorways, reminding us that amidst the tragic-comic carnival of our lives there were and are alternative places to visit—places other than the carney games and freak shows, casinos and strip joints, power-trip roller coasters and fun rides down rivers of blood.

The signs of the prophets are glowing arrows among the swarm of others that rise to the curvature of the human skull, but even though they glow, they, too must obey the gravity of human nature and come down. The prophets' visions must be quantified and analyzed, sequestered in structures and hierarchies, hammered not into ploughshares and pruning hooks, but into coins of the realm and the dire weapons of contest and domination.

Who cares? What does it matter? In the ongoing Grand Scheme, the answers are "No one" and "It doesn't." You can feel free to enter any establishment you choose in that raging metropolis out there. You can pay your money for whatever turns you on, and you can rest assured it will have no effect, one way or the other, on the next, silent, Big Bang.

I'm no prophet, but if I were one, here's what my sign would say in that city of the night: "IT'S YOUR LIFE. THE CHOICES ARE UP TO YOU."

If it's prophets you're looking for, all you have to do is look around you. They're easy to spot. They're those odd humans who choose to live by the kinder side of human nature. They'll go out of their way for you. They don't seem to care much about who gets to be in charge. They don't carry briefcases stuffed with maps and rules for you to follow. They don't offer rewards and punishments, mandatory guidebooks to a life hereafter. They tend to be quiet, unassuming, generous people.

There's something else about them that's often a dead giveaway: When the arrows come back down from the ceiling of the skull, prophets are apt to be the first to get hit.

RITUALS

Can we do without rituals in our lives? I don't think so, but maybe your experiences tell you different. I, anyway, find myself doing certain things at certain times in certain ways, and I feel I'm adrift if I lose these fixed points. Are these things, often trivial and with meaning only to me, habits rather than rituals? My wandering mind, which these days roams on its roundabout journeys with my full permission, has just inquired why it is that nuns, handmaidens of ritual, wear habits. Now I'll never be able to look at a nun—not that I'm ever likely to set eyes on one again in this lifetime—without seeing a creature of habit.

Oh, Language, Language, Language! Such a tyrant you are! You insist that we try to stuff our infinite number of infinitely varied thoughts and feelings and experiences into the inadequate little boxes you have to offer. What's more, you decree, upon pain of our being branded as simple or foolish or certifiable, that if we can't cram the contents of our minds into your containers, if it spills all over the place, then it must be fantasy or delusion; we'd best get ourselves to a psychiatrist and shrink it all until it fits. Well, to hell with that! My feet have long since grown too big to shoehorn into baby booties, thank you. For the last stretch of this hike I'm on, I'll wear the footwear I damn well please—soft, sloppy, untied and all. And don't bother nagging at me that I'm going to trip over my laces.

Now that that's off my sunken chest, I feel better. I always feel better when I'm in The Land Beyond Words, even though, of course, words can't describe it. When I'm there, I know I'm in touch with Reality—exactly the thing a psychiatrist would probably tell me I'm *out* of touch with.

I begin my early mornings with a ritual cigarette and mug of coffee, just as the sun is making its appearance over the still-dark hills to the east. I agree that smoking's a "habit," and coffee's a "habit," but not that particular, first, cigarette of the morning. Nor, for that matter, the one that I light up with my first slug of Bushmill's Irish whiskey in the evening as the hills to the west are now darkening. Those two smokes, to my way of thinking, count as rituals. That first Bushmill's, by the way, comes after my habitual, late-afternoon, long soak in the tub. This afternoon's soak was longer than usual. I lay there thinking about how to go on with our conversation. Is my tub time another habitual ritual? Whatever you want to call it is fine by me, and I won't quibble. The label that goes on the outside of a box doesn't change its contents, does it?

My guess is that rituals must have begun as observances of time's passage. I'd like so much for you to know that time doesn't do any such thing as "pass." If I could find a way to give you that knowledge, I'd relieve you of so much anxiety, so much violence, so much dread. All that's captured in those elegant little instruments on our wrists, or, for much of the world's population, in the booming of great iron bells and brass gongs, is only a clue—such an important clue!—to how the human mind is made, what it's able to see and not see. In The Flow, time simply *isn't*. There's no such thing. Out there, it's always *now*, it's always . . . well, *always*. And so, too, are the mutually attracting vibrations that have come together to compose the unique symphony that, to your ears, is "you." *You* are now, and *you* are always. If you could believe that, know that, come to *feel* that it is so, you'd have overthrown the tyrant of Time—and of Language as well. You'd be free.

It may seem that I'm off on one of my rambles and straying from our talk of rituals, but I don't think I am. As I said, I think rituals began as punctuation marks, indicating the starts and stops and pauses and exclamations in the paragraph of "time." But how can you punctuate a paragraph whose meaning is illusory? I suppose any way we want to. We can even make the punctuation marks, themselves, the meaning—and maybe that's just what's happened.

The first punctuation mark I can call up from my childhood is bedtime with the fall of night—the opening of a pair of parentheses that would close with my waking up in the morning. Time out.

In my family, the ritual of the opening parenthesis consisted of prayers, a bedtime story, a kiss, and lights out. What went on after the ritual, between the parentheses of going to sleep and waking up, was hardly incidental, as parentheses are supposed to indicate. The sadness and the terrors that occurred between them were often more immediate, fiercer and seemed more real than anything that went on outside them. We had no ritual for the closing of the parenthesis when I opened my eyes to the daylight. I didn't crawl into my parents' bed, for instance. They didn't share one. I can remember my mother and father in separate beds in the same room, and then, later, they slept in separate bedrooms.

I'm on my second Bushmill's as I write this. I didn't have a good day today, and I'll probably have two more slugs of the stuff before I lie down to open tonight's parenthesis. I learned earlier that a dear friend, who's in our local hospital, has slipped into a coma. In addition to the emptiness and sadness I feel at the prospect of losing her companionship—I have hardly any companions left now—it's more on my mind than usual that this could be the night that my own parenthesis fails to close in the morning. I may not see tomorrow's first light seep into the meadow, bringing gray definition to the uniform darkness. It may be left to my neighbors' eyes to see the monochrome meadow slowly flood and then drown in color. If tonight's not the night, another soon will be. Anne and I—she's my friend in the coma—had a ritual we always performed with our initial cocktail. We'd raise our glasses to each other and say the old, familiar, Irish toast: "The first today . . . in *this* hand." It got to be a habit.

The whiskey is making me feel Einstein-ish, and I'll give you a Bushmill-brilliant equation: Light and dark are the sum of the ways that planets move, divided by human perception. That may be one of those evening dresses that shimmer by candlelight, but look pretty shabby stumbling home at dawn. But seeing as how there may not be a dawn for me tomorrow, who cares?

Here's what I think I'm trying to say. We talk of the moon's light and dark sides, its hot and cold sides, as though those were things that hunk of stuff up there really possessed, in and of itself, without us spinning here on the sidelines, giving what we can see and feel names that suit ourselves. There's no more light and dark out there in The Flow than there is time. But the way we're constructed makes that a notion that's awkward for us to work with. What's really going on up there on the moon looks a certain way to us Earthlings, and we talk about night and day. Whatever words we use, they say more about us and our construction than they do about the goings-on up there *or* down here. To help us make sense out of our jabberwocky about light and dark and heat and cold, we punctuate. Most of us do put night into parentheses, but not all of us. People on nightshifts don't. If owls could punctuate, they wouldn't, either.

Early humans could see many events in their lives that reoccurred. Perhaps it was trying to keep track of their comings and goings that gave rise to the notion of Time and to the idea that to get from one reoccurring event to the next, Time had to "pass." Some events reoccurred less frequently than others, and those events most likely seemed more important than the rapid, predictable round of night and day. Such things as the seasons, the sowing of seeds, the gathering of the harvest, called out for exclamation marks rather than mundane periods. "Wow! A bumper crop!" Or, on the other hand, "Shit! Another hungry winter!" Depending on the situation, an exclamation mark could look like a little explosion at the bottom with a rocket shooting up above it. Then it was time for a binge of music and dance, drunkenness and fornication. Oh, happy days! Other times, the form of the exclamation mark was more like slender, sinister dagger with a drop of blood at the end of its sharp point. Time to sacrifice another virgin! But whatever their aspect, the exclamatory rituals punctuated the nonsense paragraph of Time and gave the illusion of its passing some meaning.

The first exclamation marks in my life were, I think, my birthdays. I don't suppose any of us remember our earliest ones. I certainly don't. I can remember blurs of balloons, smears of ice cream and cake, but nothing more. Somewhere in a box that's somewhere in this house, I think I have a faded, grainy, black-and-white photograph of what may have been my third birthday party. If I ever found it, it wouldn't mean a thing to me. I wouldn't know who took it, who the people in it were, and I'd certainly feel no association with that little person at the center of attention. All the same, I like the idea of that photograph. It would be worth any thousand—or ten thousand—words that I could write about rituals as an attempt to give substance to the insubstantial. It would be a picture of me, but not of who I am, of people that no longer exist, and of a moment no one remembers. The photo lies somewhere in a dark box in a dark cupboard. I could, of course, make it a part of "now" again. I could dig it out, hold it in my hands and send its image to my "now" brain. But it would mean nothing, nothing at all.

So many birthdays have come and gone, and yet I remember few specific ones. Looking back, I can re-evoke feelings of excitement, elation and mystification. The excitement came, I think, from all the family drumbeating that went on as the day got nearer and nearer. The elation came from . . . Aha! Thank you, Bushmill's! You've just opened a door I didn't know was there: There *wasn't* any elation. There was only the feeling that I was *supposed* to feel elated. As for the feeling of mystification that comes back to me now, it must have come partly from wondering why I was supposed to feel elated, and partly from wondering why, on that particular day when my numbers changed, I didn't feel any different than I had the day before.

There must have been at least one birthday when I actually got a present that I'd really been longing for. You'd think I'd remember a moment like that, wouldn't you? But none comes to mind.

Did the exclamation marks of my birthdays shoot up like rockets? Or did they thrust down like daggers? They don't seem to have had the impact of either. Chances are that, as for most children, they probably contained elements of both in their frenzies and disappointments. But thinking of daggers and blood has just rescued one birthday moment out of oblivion. Don't ask me how old I was, because I have no idea, but we were playing a game called Bullet Pudding. What you did was pack flour into a bowl and then turn the form out, carefully, onto the table. On top of the flour mound, you set a gumdrop. Each person had to take a turn cutting a slice out of the mound. Sooner or later, of course, it had to collapse, gumdrop and all. Whoever had cut that final slice had to pick the gumdrop out of the floury wreckage by the teeth, hands behind back. And as that person made the ritual act of penance, the fun was to push his or her face deep into the flour so that it came up white as a ghost. HA HA HA! To us children, it was funniest of all when it happened to a grownup.

On this occasion, that penance fell to my mother. When she bent over to get the gumdrop in her teeth, I gleefully pounced on her head, and in doing so, managed to split her upper lip wide open against the tabletop. The flour on her face turned red. I went to my room in terror and in tears.

Christmas and Easter came to our house as other exclamation marks. I found Christmas more and more burdensome the older I got. Once Santa was unbearded, the whole affair, starting earlier each year, became increasingly like a circus elephant run amok—an elephant dressed in a ridiculous tutu with a crucifix swinging from its neck. I liked Easter a lot better. By the time Easter came, it was warm where we were living, and the world smelled of hyacinths.

Thanksgiving I liked, and I still do. I'm deeply thankful for the friends I still have, and I take the opportunity Thanksgiving brings to let them know how grateful I am. There are nine of us now who, for years, have been getting together at Thanksgiving. The ritual is unvarying—and highly ritualized. I provide the locale and the liquids, and each person brings the same dish each year. No transgressions are permitted. No changes in the menu, no monkey-business with the recipes. We usually end up being ten or 11 at table, because we always hope for a stray or two who have nowhere particular to go. The strays, however, are not allowed to bring food.

Our core group began 12 strong. Three have died, taking along with them their signature dishes. We've agreed that we're not allowed to replicate those dishes. It's our acknowledgment that our friends who made them are irreplaceable. Instead of saying a grace of some kind, we spend a moment missing those who used to nourish both our lives and our tummies. We fondly remember, for instance, Martha's wry, but never cruel, observations on how our town is being run, or ruined, and by whom. We miss her oddly pickled beets. Next Thanksgiving, it looks like our group will be only eight and doing without Anne's irrepressible, bawdy humor and her string beans *au gratin*. She was the one who first made us laugh at the inevitable outcome of our self-imposed ritual: Some Thanksgiving to come, she said, there'll be only one of us left, sitting roofless by the side of the road, with a couple of homeless hobos for company, eating cranberry sauce out of a can and with nothing to drink.

My thoughts of Thanksgivings past don't come with the jab of an exclamation mark. They feel more like, maybe, a semi-colon—a distinct pause that needs reflection both on the completeness of what's gone before and the required dependence upon it of what follows.

For me, Thanksgiving's different than, say, Christmas or Easter in another way as well. Though it may mark an historical event at which we weren't present—you know, the Pilgrims and all that—the gathering in of the harvest in the fall is still as real and current an event as the reoccurrence of tax day every April 15. This leads me to lump Thanksgiving in with things like bar mitzvahs, graduations, weddings and funerals. Like birthday rituals, the rituals that mark these moments punctuate our actual and ongoing lives. Come to think of it, it seems a bit strange to me that we don't have a ritual to celebrate birth itself. There are, of course, ceremonies that immediately follow a birth, that initiate the new being into the particular culture it's dropped into. I don't like these rituals. They remind me of all those early explorers who ran about the world planting flags all over the place, saying "This turf's ours!"—regardless of who happened to be already living there at the time. But as for celebrating birth itself? Did you ever hear someone say, "Sorry, I can't come to dinner on Thursday. I'm going to a birthfest"?

I feel ambivalent about coming-of-age punctuations. They usually give me that fudge-the-issue feeling of quotation marks when used to indicate "so to speak." Let's celebrate! You've become, so to speak, "mature." I'd feel better about them if they out-and-out marked a human's ability to reproduce with no beating about the bush. I can see celebrating a boy's first squirt, the older males dancing up a storm and shouting, "Welcome to the club!" I dealt with my first squirt in whispers to a couple of trusted peers . . . who sniggered. A girl's first period must often be alarming and the source of behind-the-door, conspiratorial huddles with her mother. There's the ritual somewhere, though I can't remember where, for a mother to slap her daughter's face when she has her first period, as if to indicate to the daughter that she's gone and done something shameful. What kind of punctuation is that supposed to be?

When it comes to coming of age, I'd happily lift a glass in a straightforward, civil ceremony of some kind where the elders took a youngster aside and laid it on the line. "We've decided that now that you've lived for this arbitrary number of years, we're going to let you drive a car, vote, buy cigarettes and get drunk in public. In return, we're going to hold you responsible for the babies you make, the bills you run up, and anyone you run over."

As for weddings, I stay away from them if I can, unless they're in the bureau of a Justice of the Peace or in a registry office. I like the feeling of the plain, functional, worn furniture in such places. The tone it provides seems to me totally appropriate to the matter at hand. If a chair is well made, it can stand a lot of wear and tear.

People's choice of punctuation for a funeral seems to resemble something between whatever that string of little periods is called and a question mark. Their choices naturally tend to reflect the consensus of the cultures they live— and die—in, but, of course, they don't always do so. The group's consensus doesn't necessarily satisfy the wrestling each individual inevitably does with the problem of what comes next. A person's struggle to find a satisfying, reassuring and convincing answer isn't made any easier by the abundance of conflicting cultural opinions about the matter.

The whole issue is made murkier still by having so many of those opinions offered not as opinions but rather as certainties. Certainty, of course, is what everyone's looking for and hopes to find. But when there are so many options, and each is presented as the one-and-only, mutually exclusive, true and definitive account of what comes next, certainty turns itself inside out and swallows itself. It burps and re-emerges as *un*certainty. The claim to being right about the matter is the one claim that reveals the sham. There's no way to have multiple one-and-onlies.

It's seems odd that the compulsion toward certainty is so strong that those of one persuasion will fight to the death with those of another persuasion, eagerly sending one another off to find out the truth of the matter for themselves. Well, there's no substitute for firsthand experience, is there? The trouble is that no one, so far, has bothered to report back what the truth is.

So, some people end up punctuating funerals with the series of dots that indicate the dead continue on in some way, while others, understandably perplexed, settle for a question mark about whether they go on somewhere or not. The one punctuation mark that most of you seem to avoid like the plague is a period—otherwise known as a full stop. Death cannot be the end of the story. There *has* to be more. Which is correct. There *is* more, and full stops have no place, not in The Flow. I'm in a bind here, because I don't want to seem to be tossing into the arena yet another alternative "certainty" for everyone to fight and die over. But how am I to proceed?

The telephone is ringing. A confused telemarketer in Bombay? I wish! At this hour, it's bound to be bad news. Most likely about Anne, I'd guess. I'll be right back.

*   *   *

Yes, Anne has died. We will, indeed, be eight for Thanksgiving—that is, providing *I* get that far. It seems a long way off, Thanksgiving, and I can feel my body rhythms changing. They're not as tightly woven together as they once were. My memory is an unreliable record of the whats and whens and wheres of my life. When I run the film backwards now, there are double images and blank frames. If I don't make lists of the things I need to get and do, if I don't write down the appointments I said I'd keep, they all get washed away by the incoming tide. I'm forever wondering what it was I came into the kitchen for, where I set down the screwdriver I had five minutes ago. Yesterday, I blistered my fingers taking a saucepan of soup off the stove without a potholder. The burn didn't reach my brain for a full three seconds.

I'm unraveling is what I'm doing. I don't feel frayed as much as I feel made up of loose parts, connections that are separating, bolts and joints that are working themselves free. I have friends in the same boat. They feel frustrated and frightened. They feel the boat is leaking, sinking. I wish they could know, as I do, that our bodies are simply getting ready to rejoin The Flow from which they coalesced. If they could know that, they'd feel what I feel: a calm elation at the prospect of blending back into the magnificence of it all.

I know what the amalgamation called Anne has become, and I know what I will become as well. I know it because I know where I came from, where we all come from. I know the "coming" from firsthand experience. As for the transition that's approaching me, no, I have no firsthand experience of that, and I won't be back to tell you about it when I do. I won't have any "experience" of the aftermath to tell you about. To have such experience, my body functions would have to continue on as they are, keeping my senses intact to record what's happening. I'd need an ongoing brain to process the information, not to mention some new-fangled kind of cell phone to report home with. Actually, in addition to a new-fangled cell phone, I'd need a new-fangled brain to go with it. This current brain of mine wouldn't do me much good; it doesn't get along with cell phones. The other day, Jason, the retired stockbroker down the road, lent me his cell phone to make a call. Somewhere in the process, stupid me hit "erase all" by mistake, sending his entire list of contacts into the ether. Gone. Like Anne.

It's time for another Bushmill's. And a "Here's to you dear Anne. The first one today in *this* hand!"

(Lucky Kali with all those hands to put Bushmill's in! From my long stay in India, I remember her as The Ferocious Mother goddess, but as I recall, she was supposed to free us from the fear of death as well. How appropriate!)

Back to our talk about "certainty," specifically, how on Earth—Earth with a capital E, that is—I can let you know what it is *I* know without adding to all the *un*certainty by staking out yet another "certain" claim.

Doesn't feeling certain about something require that there be something certain to feel certain about? But pause a moment. Doesn't it also imply that there's a possibility, even a remote one, that there's some doubt, even just a shred, about that something's certainty? I can stand out there in the field in a downpour, and I can say to you, "I'm certain it's raining." Of course I can say that, given that I'm drenched to the bone, but I think you'd look at me more strangely if I said that than if I'd simply said "It's raining." It would be different, though, if I stood there and said to you, "One thing's for certain; I could use an umbrella right now." It would be different, because I wouldn't be making a comment about the rain that is outside me, all around me, but quite indifferent to me. Instead, I'd be making a comment about *me,* giving you an insider's view of my feelings, expressing concern about myself, and telling you I'd rather be dry.

Someone else might feel differently about the rain. I remember walking through the streets of New York City late one summer afternoon when, seemingly out of nowhere, down came a torrential deluge. I took shelter in a doorway. People hurried past me, scowling. There were natty, three-piece-suitors with briefcases and newspapers held over their heads. A pair of young women skittered by—pert, perfectly primped. "My shoes!" said one. "My *hair!*" said the other.

I stood there in my doorway, and though it wasn't nice, everyone's discomfort was making me smile. Then along came a kid, hop-skipping-jumping through the puddles, water sheeting down his face, tee shirt and shorts plastered to his skinny body. Our looks met in a sort of conspiracy. "Man!" he said. "Isn't this *great?*"

Different certainties about the same "something." That something was the rain, just doing its non-human thing and raining.

Astronomers sift through the stars, looking for certainty. One finds certainty here, another finds certainty there. Their certainties collide. In an eruption of genial doubt? Usually not, judging from what I read in the newspapers. The opposing intellects dig in even deeper to defend their turf. It can get nasty. The ritual of the Nobel Prize may be at stake.

Different certainties about the same "something." That something is The Flow, just doing its non-human thing and flowing. Neither certainty nor doubt have any meaning out there, any more than does Time. Far from offering you yet another, rival certainty to add to the confusion, I'm trying here to leave you with a glimpse of a place from which you and your sojourn here look different. I remember being told in science class that whoever invented the lever said, "Give me a place to stand, and I could move the Earth." *That's* the place I want you to see.

Choose whatever color, shape, size or make of umbrella you want to keep yourself dry. Argue about which is best, if you want to. Use them to poke each other's eyes out, if that's your way. Or make room under yours for someone who doesn't have one. What I want to help you feel, to understand, to come to *know*, to embrace and to *trust*, is that however you order your umbrella affairs among yourselves, it doesn't matter to the rain.

Half past one in the morning???? Can it really be? And does it matter, anyway? Yes, it matters, but only to me. I could make it matter to my neighbors, if I had any nearby, by cranking up the stereo and blasting some Heavy Metal out into the darkness, yanking them out of their peaceful parentheses of sleep. "Turn that goddam noise off!" they'd shout. "What's the matter with you? Don't you know it's half past one in the morning?"

But there's only me within earshot, me and the you I imagine sitting in that chair over there. If you're someone reading this, it may be four in the afternoon where you are for all I know. Or maybe no one's reading this. If somebody writes something and there's no one there to read it, do the written ideas really exist? There's something wrong with that proposition. It doesn't work as well as the tree falling with no one there to hear it, does it? I know what's wrong with it: the empty part of the Bushmill's bottle, that's what. I'm not drunk, mind you, but I'm not exactly sober, either. And I've still got an inch left in my glass and damned if I'll waste it.

I wonder why drunks stare into their drinks the way they do. What are they seeing there? All I see in my glass right now is amber liquid and the last vestige of an ice cube. Hey, here's a thought: If it's true that no two snowflakes are ever exactly the same, then I suppose no two ice cubes are, either. Awesome! There they are in their tidy, plastic trays, all gelling nicely, looking just alike, but each one turning into something different. And where do ice cubes and snowflakes go when they melt? Some, I suppose, seep into the ground and others evaporate up into the sky and then fall into the ocean. That means they're still around in some form, that there's no getting rid of them.

The ice cube I'm staring at is melting into my drink, and my drink's going to go into me. And then out of me and through pipes to who-knows-where, to become . . . . See? There they are, the four little dots in a string that leave the conclusion open-ended. Dot dot dot dot. I think I'll name this ice cube "Anne." And bottoms up.

Now it's definitely time for my ritual brushing of the teeth, implants and all. Come to think of it, maybe I'll skip that ritual tonight. In fact, if you don't mind, I think I'll open tonight's parenthesis right there on the recliner. I'd rather be in my bed, but it seems a challenging distance to travel at the moment. And there'd be all the business of undressing and hanging things up.

Yes, the recliner will do fine. I can certainly get that far, and the only things I'll have to worry about hanging up are my spurs. If I do, I'll leave it to someone else to take off my clothes.

You And I

This farewell love letter has been a while in the writing. Good heavens, the siege of Baghdad has long since become past history! It's aftermath, though, still fills the evening news with mounting body counts not only in Iraq, but, as of yesterday, in London. Differently crafted arrows of Truth and Righteousness are raining down from the cupola of the human skull as they're bound to do, killing the archers and bystanders without distinction.

Yes, my conversation with you over there in that ratty, overstuffed chair has gone on longer that I thought it would, and for you, perhaps, too long. As for me, our time together has been a joy—except that my toes are sore from stubbing against words.

I woke up feeling strange the day before yesterday. It was similar to the feeling I've sometimes had with a hangover, a feeling that I was outside myself, watching me go through the usual morning movements. But there was a difference this time. There was none of a hangover's prickly-blanket feeling. Quite the opposite. Part of me was sharply distinct from the rest, and that part had the brilliant clarity of cold, clear water. Come to think of it, that part of me felt it *was* the water, and the creature shuffling about making coffee was only a fish swimming about within it. The feeling lasted well through the morning until I'd begun wondering whether this might be how the rest of my days would continue, and whether I'd better begin getting used to it. When my split personality glued itself together again around noon, I felt relieved to be back in one piece in this world that has become familiar to me—relieved, but at the same time deprived. It was like I'd been allowed to hold something beautiful, precious and fragile in my hands for a moment and then had it taken away.

A sudden memory: I'm remembering how, as I child, I was once allowed to hold a spray of jade flowers. It lived on a table in the living room of a rather grand lady my parents would sometimes go to visit. Whenever they'd take me with them—with stern warnings to be on my best behavior—I'd go to that table and peer at the jade confection, moving my head slowly this way and that, watching the light as it changed coming through the curves of the thin, translucent foliage. One day the lady asked me if I'd like to hold it. I nodded, and she placed it in my hands. What delight! What terror! When she took it back from me, my relief was enormous, and right alongside it was an enormous desire to hold that marvel again.

Unlike in that memory, I felt no terror in my altered state the day before yesterday, no fear, not even anxiety. You might have, though. You might have been afraid you were losing your mind and come out of it hoping you'd never have such a weird feeling again. I don't blame you; that's the kind of episode that makes rational people seek help. As for me, I was simply awed by such a tangible experience—Ouch! Just stubbed my toe again on a touchable untouchable! To hell with it. As I was saying, such a tangible experience of me as The Flow and me as the you that you feel yourself to be. I'm hoping that feeling will come back again. It was a tantalizing glimpse of the celestial celebration to which I'll so soon be returning. The episode left me elated.

It did something else, too. It made me want to read, for the first time all at once, these many pages I've gone and written to you. And so, yesterday, that's what I went and did. I took the pages, not to the hammock by the pond, where I knew I'd soon go doggish and fall asleep, but to a flatish stone on the rise beyond the pond. It's a place with a pleasant view back to the house, and a perch where, though its form nicely cups the boney cheeks of my bottom, I have to stay awake or fall over. I read and I read. What I found was that, for the most part, what I want so much to tell you is here, but I knew it was here in words and sentences and paragraphs, ideas and images, whose fullness of meaning, whose resonance, could only be heard by me, myself. I felt all I'd been able to do was force a rich stew through a strainer and offer you some thin broth. On several occasions while reading, I imagined my patient, stalwart printer sticking out its white tongue at me again and again as if to say: "Thought you had something to say, did you? Well, here's all you get."

I don't know about you, but I'm comfortable with ambivalence, even grateful for it. We have few feelings that aren't tempered by their opposites, and to try to deny that is to falsify a feeling altogether. Reading these pages, I knew I'd failed to break out of my skull, and that I'd fail to break through into yours. That was a disappointment. The disappointment was eased, however, by the knowledge that no one has ever succeeded in staging such a jailbreak, let alone breaking into the Fort Knox of another person's mind. But I felt satisfied that I'd tried. The trying was enough. And it seemed possible to me that the effort might at least open a tiny chink somewhere in the fortress wall, a chink through which could seep air carrying the scent of blossoms from a world beyond.

It was only when I finished reading what I'd written that I thought to add this little chapter. With the end of the last page had come a feeling of: "Okay, but so what? What does it all add up to?" Part of me said it was just what it was and didn't have to add up to anything, so why worry? Another part of me, on the other hand, began looking for what bound it all together, for what, if anything, was common to it all. Only last night, pouring my second Bushmill's, did an answer take shape. It was all about "You and I." (Yes, yes, I know it's supposed to be you and *me*, but I put the both of us inside quotation marks to bind us together, rather than leaving us dangling as separate objects of a preposition.) By "You and I," I don't mean only the me that's writing and the you that's reading. I mean any "me" out there, anyone who stakes a claim to being an "I" and approaches the world with that singular point of view. That's everyone, isn't it? I think it is, even editors and Royalty and people with multiple personalities. As for the "you," that's everyone that isn't "I," and, at least in English, "you" is conveniently both singular and plural.

Why do you and I have such trouble together, here on this tiny speck of stuff spinning around through space? Do we have to? Will we always? Almost certainly, yes. *Almost* certainly.

That "almost" leaves a little wriggling space—not much, but that's more than none at all. The obvious question is: What would it take to make that space wider, wide enough for human beings to wriggle through into a new order of things where peace and plenty prevailed, where money was merely the convenience it started out to be, where blood was something to guard zealously within the body, instead of wantonly spraying it around. What indeed! Some genetic engineering? Not unless the genetic engineers had already wriggled through the tiny space into the new, enlightened order, leaving behind human ambition, self-interest, greed, and the hunger for power.

No, that's not going to work. The genetic engineers are already among us, and they're no different from anyone else. How about a visitation from outer space that suddenly binds humans together as comrades in the face of something "other," something alien? Writers and film makers galore have played with that fantasy, goodness knows, and blood ends up everywhere.

What more human characteristic is there than the dislike of the unlike? That particular piece of baggage is *much* too big to squeeze through the wriggle space, no matter how wide it gets.

Yes, the obvious question is how to make the space bigger, but you don't have to live nearly as long as I have to know that the obvious question often isn't the one that that brings the answer to a problem. Flight didn't get off the ground by trying to answer the obvious question of how to build a device lighter than air that gravity wouldn't pull down. Someone, eventually, had to ask what it was about thin air that could pull heavy things *up*. What a cockamamie notion!

Well, then, the next obvious question is: If we can't make the wriggle space bigger, big enough to let us and our baggage through, how can we make ourselves and our baggage smaller? To most people, that will come as another cockamamie idea. Isn't the whole object of the game to make ourselves as big as we can? As smart and strong and dominant and rich and powerful as we can? Who on earth wants to be *smaller*? The answer, of course, is not much of anyone. For people to start wanting to feel smaller rather than bigger, we'd have to change human nature, wouldn't we? Could we do that? A glance at history should let the penny drop. Asking how to change human nature is another obvious question that won't give us an answer to the problems you and I have with one another. Looking for ways to be smaller may well be a cockamamie notion, but the trouble is, it isn't cockamamie enough.

So then, what? If we can't widen the wriggle space to let us through, and we can't make ourselves small enough to let us pass, we're stuck where we are. You and I are going to have to go on duke-ing it out. (Is that how you spell it? "Duking" certainly looks stupid.)

What is it we fight about, anyway, you and I? Oh, I know, we fight over money and land and water and food and one another's "significant others," but those are the bells that ring when you pull on the ropes. It's the ropes themselves that I want to get tangled up in here, and cursed by words, you know that tangled up is what I'll be. Never mind. If we've gotten this far, we can tangle one more time. "It takes two to tangle," as they say. (Sorry, I couldn't resist that one and didn't want you to think I'm so doddery that it didn't occur to me.)

We fight over superiority, that's for sure, and we fight over it in lots of different ways. There's a whole bunch of bells at the end of *that* rope! But suppose instead of saying, "Mine is bigger than yours," or "Mine is better than yours," we could learn to say, "Mine is *different* than yours." What would we have to fight about then? Wouldn't we have to agree? We might even get interested in each other's differences and find ways to enjoy them. They might brighten up the grayness of my being the same, boring, old me. Mind you, I'm not saying that's what people *should* do, only that it's something they *could* do. They could also find faster, more efficient ways to go about ethnic cleansing, reducing the innumerable differences we fight over down to the difference between those who think ethnic cleansing is a good idea and those who don't.

We fight over responsibility and blame. We do a lot of that. You hold me responsible because my people, sometime in the past, killed a lot of your people. Suppose we each took responsibility, and held one another responsible, only for what we did in our lifetimes—at least from some "age of responsibility" onwards? Blame me for killing your husband or raping your wife, fine, but don't blame me for Dad's alcoholic spree in the Thunderbird that left you an orphan. Should I be held responsible for my people having kept your people in slavery all those years? Some people act as though they think so. We could decide that what dead people did in their lifetimes was their responsibility and the responsibility died along with them. We could start from the premise that each of us begins with a clean slate. We *could* look at life and one another that way. We don't have to mix responsibility and blame in with semen and eggs—not if we decide we don't like the taste of that particular omelet. (Oh, yuk! What a gross metaphor!) On the other hand, sure, we can subscribe to the notion that fairness does indeed demand that the sins of the fathers require penance from the unborn of generations to come. That's another possible way to organize things.

Now *that's* something that keeps us busy fighting all the time, isn't it? Social organization. I know I wandered about tripping over the dead and wounded on that battlefield a while ago, but I wasn't thinking about "you and I" then. Where it seems to me that you and I often come to grief is, absurdly, over something accidental—into what kind of social organization we were accidentally born. Whatever kind it was, we certainly didn't choose it, and yet we find ourselves defending it, poised in a boxer's stance, ready for fisticuffs with any challenger.

I'm a big fan of those British period pieces that turn up on Public Television—you know, *Upstairs Downstairs* and all the others it pulled along in its wake. What a world those people lived in! Strange and artificial as that world seemed to most of us, we quickly acclimatized to its conventions, suspended our judgmental inclinations toward modern-day political correctness, and accepted that in that time and place the way those people behaved and organized themselves was, to them, the *only* way to go about things. There were those who were born to be masters, and there were those who were born to be servants. Everyone knew that. No one questioned it. Upward mobility? I doubt the phrase even existed—any more, say, than "leveraged buyout."

Human nature wasn't any different then than it is nowadays, only the way the *You*'s and *I*'s of that time organized their interactions. We couldn't have had such a rollicking good time watching those stories from the past unfold if they hadn't been packed with the familiar cannon fodder of greed and jealousy, rivalry and deception, and, of course, sex. But everyone knew his or her place. *Sex* knew its place. Upstairs, the place was amidst silken sheets and downy pillows. Downstairs, it was the prickly hay of a stall in the stable. Did sex stay in its place? Of course not. Sex never stays in its place. All I said was it *knew* its place.

What I'm getting at here is that shaped by the context of our own lives, we find it a hard leap to accept that in other times and in other places people did and do organize things differently, and that to them, their customs and conventions seem as natural, appropriate and inevitable as ours do to us. If we could slip into their shoes for a time—that is, assuming shoes are a part of their culture—we'd be able to share their comfortable familiarity with their odd-looking footwear, their certainty that how their shoes are made is the way shoes *ought* to be made, and their belligerent resistance to trying any other model.

For once that's not such a bad analogy. Where I live, as in many other places these days, there's an ever-increasing population of new immigrants. The shoes their children are growing up wearing are very different from the shoes their parents were wearing when they arrived in this country. Manuel, who keeps this place from being overrun by nature and chops my firewood, arrived from Managua, Nicaragua, about ten years ago. He was quickly followed by his pregnant wife and three-year-old son. A year later his elderly, widowed father joined them. Last year, Manuel did me the honor of inviting me to his daughter's birthday party. There was the grandfather, wearing highly polished, square-toed leather shoes below the cuffs of his neatly pressed, beige pants. Manuel, in clean, faded jeans, was wearing new, yellowish laborer's boots. His wife was so immaculately turned out that you couldn't believe she ever does a day's work in her life, let alone does the unpleasant parts of a day's work for several other people as well. Her perfect, pearlescent toenails emerged from dainty, plastic, grass-green shoes with thin straps around the ankle and the kind of high, spiky heels you don't see much anymore. Fernando, their now teen-aged son who prefers to be called Frank, looked well-scrubbed and not too happy about it. Below a clean, purple tee shirt with Spiderman on it, he had a pair of gravity-defying, baggy semi-jeans that hovered as if my magic between the cleft of his butt and the calves of his legs. His white socks ended in a pair of . . . well, I don't know what they're called these days. They certainly weren't "sneakers." They were heavily padded, boat-like things that appeared to be twice the size of his feet, and on their sterns, flashing yellow lights.

It was an affair that managed to stay festive despite what seemed to me a lot of bickering within the family. The grandfather speaks no English, but his ongoing critical comments—from what I could pick up, mainly about his daughter-in-law's Americanized cooking and his grandson's deportment—were unmistakable. Manuel and his wife speak some English, but twice at the birthday party Frank felt embarrassed enough by their grammar that he had to correct them, with apologetic glances at me. Frank, himself, sounds like any American kid and speaks minimal Spanish, though he understands plenty enough to know what to do when he's told to, and that most of the time he's doing it wrong.

A clever animator could have turned the whole event into a cultural dispute among their shoes.

From my odd point of view, none of this means anything—or at least means only that the *I*'s and *You*'s out there are so embedded in their separate, accidental contexts that they'll even fight to the death with one another over whose context should prevail. Had we lived when slavery was the norm, most of us would like to think that we'd have been among the first to speak out against it. I doubt that would have been so. We'd have had no perspective to bring to slavery other than the one from which we'd been conditioned, from birth, to perceive and understand the world around us. That perspective would have included the unquestioning acceptance that the natural order of things relegated certain kinds of people to certain kinds of pigeonholes. Most of us would, indeed, have been unable to see the forest for the trees, even if the trees had bodies hanging from their limbs.

Perspective. Somewhere in these ramblings, I know I've batted that word around before, but I didn't realize until right this minute that "perspective" was perhaps the closest words will let me get to naming the object around which these pages have been making their eccentric orbits. Never mind "wriggle room." In fact, I'm going to wriggle my way out of that clumsy metaphor here and now. We're not camels trying to squeeze through a needle's eye. Far from it. The "known universe" offers us more space than we know what to do with, and there's a lot more space beyond that. To resolve the most important issues that divide all of us *You*'s and *I*'s from one another, we don't need to change who we are, only to look at ourselves in a different way, from a different perspective—from the disinterested perspective of the uncaring Flow. That perspective is the truest view of humans' place in the scheme of things. You'll challenge that assertion, I know. I can see you rising indignantly out of your chair over there and taking up a boxer's stance, ready to duke it out with me.

Sorry, but I can't oblige you. You'll get no duke-ing back from this old man—not even arguments or protests. Trying to convince you of anything is not what these pages have been about. I've written them because I've loved you, and I didn't want to leave you without telling you what I know. If you have to go on punching out one another's reflections in curvy, fun-house mirrors, go for it. All I can say is that from my perspective, it looks odd and unnecessary.

And dangerous. We both know how badly shattered glass can cut, don't we? I will be sad for you when I see the scarlet proof of *that* reality yet again tonight on the evening news.

THE SONG'S LAST NOTES

Here I sit, my head leaning against the reedy shore, and I have sung my first and (almost) last.

No one may ever hear my song, and that doesn't bother me at all. I didn't sing it for it to be heard; I sang it because it welled up in my throat and needed to be set free. I have loved you, and this song is the form my love has taken. Never mind the lyrics. I've said all along that I find words tricky, slippery, fickle, deceptive, shape-shifting kinds of things, only able to convey shadowy approximations of the fullness of a thought or a feeling. I think of the times I've woken from a dream, flooded and stunned by the intensity of the dream experience and wanting, so badly, to share what I felt with someone else. But trying to put my dream feelings into words was like my pointing to cinders floating in the air, vainly hoping they could evoke the experience of a roaring fire.

I can hear the voice of my mother's father. Somewhere about ten, I was doing a bad job of cutting a plank that I wanted to make into something-or-other. "This saw's no good," I complained. "A bad workman blames his tools," my grandfather said. I'll accept that, but I'm older, much older now than my grandfather was then, and that, of course, makes me wiser than he was, doesn't it? Words are wretchedly inadequate, squirmy little things, whether you're clever in using them or whether you're not. And yet, we let them become our benchmarks of reality.

But if my song should be heard, if a chance breeze carries it across the pond to ears that happen to be passing by, I wonder how it will sound. Differently to different ears, I suppose, but I hope it doesn't come as a sad song. It has flowed out of affirmation and rejoicing. It has flowed out of The Flow and has taken human form as ecstasy.

Is a universe that does its thing, mindless of human affairs, a cold, unfeeling place? By now, perhaps, just perhaps, a little bird—or maybe a big bird, like a swan—is telling you that's a meaningless question. Maybe, as we've been talking together, just maybe, you've been able to gain an inkling of a different understanding of the universe. That understanding is simplicity itself, and it's that the universe is *beyond* human understanding. All that you've been taught about the universe is only instruction about that little aspect of The Flow the human brain, and the clever instruments of its invention, can describe, quantify and make available to you. It's awesome, the inventiveness of the human mind as it tries to break through the curvature of the skull. All the same, the human description of the universe *is* only an invention, a useful construction. That's part of why the question of whether it's a cold, unfeeling place is meaningless.

Another part is that what it is that is "out there," as you like to put it, is not a place. It's more like an event. A volcano exploding is an event. So are The Olympics. Events may happen in a place, but neither a volcanic explosion nor the Olympic games is, itself, a "place." As for the "cold and unfeeling" part of the question, events can generate all sorts of feelings among human beings, but it doesn't compute, Will Robinson, to talk of events having feelings of their own.

Seeing yourself as the prisoner of a cold, unfeeling universe is putting yourself in illusory confinement. There are no bars holding us in unless we choose to see them there. There is no jailer unless we create one. You and I find ourselves in a "place," that's for sure, and we certainly have feelings about it. But what we make of this place, and what feelings we have about it, are up to us. Up to each and every one of us. *Only* up to us. Up to us *alone*. Which means, up to . . . *you*. That cornucopia of choice comes with the earthly turf.

Knowing that, as I do, has been the source of my ecstasy while I've been here among you. From the earliest years I can remember, I knew that I was growing with the freedom to make of my time anything I wanted. Naturally, like any child, I grew amidst rules and regulations—rules of the road and regulations of human conduct. Within my family, I had to make my bed, put my toys away, and get my homework done. I had to say please and thank you, play nicely with other children, be polite to grownups, and not throw things at people.

For the most part, I found it easy to accept these rules of the road. They were practical and kept human traffic flowing more smoothly. Usually, the consequences of disregarding the rules brought me more inconvenience than did my observing them. I knew, all the same, that these required acts were nothing more than matters of human convenience. They had nothing to do with The Flow, the event of which I knew I was a part. If I chose to break the rules, figuring—often wrongly—that the consequences would be worth the breach, I was free to do so. There was no reason—that is, no reason beyond my own reasoning—that I couldn't do so, no reason at all.

Once I was out on my own, with my own clock to set and my own money to spend, my experience of freedom was exhilarating. There were so many games going on to choose from! There were games going on within other games. There were games that tumbled over into other games that were being played on next-door playing fields. Some of the playing fields were so large you couldn't tell where they began or ended. Rules? There was a great snarl of them, and umpires running around dropping red flags all over the place until it looked like late autumn in Vermont. The penalties the umpires imposed were a lot stiffer than those I was used to at home. Losing my paycheck hurt a lot more than losing my allowance. The one night I spent in jail didn't feel at all like being sent to my room. But if I could abide, or avoid, the umpires' penalties, observing the rules or breaking them was still up to me. There was nothing about The Flow that cared if I did the one or the other. Another glee-inspiring part of this lavish, new freedom was that, unlike living in my family, there was now more than one game in town, and I was free to change games whenever I wanted.

At first I was surprised to find that the people around me didn't feel as free as I did, and then it dawned on me: Here, in the culture I arrived in by accident, you were expected to subscribe to a kind of overall Gaming Association if you wanted to play any of the games at all. You were supposed to abide by the Association's by-laws, even if you skirted around the rules of a particular game. These greater by-laws were written in old-fashioned, copperplate handwriting. The loops and curlicues spelled out Honesty and Dishonesty, Right and Wrong, even Good and Evil.

Oh, there were folks who out-and-out bucked even The Association's by-laws. They got branded with sizzling marks like subversive, revolutionary, deviant, psychotic, amoral, or sinful. I've come across a good many such mavericks in my life. At first, when I'd meet one, I'd think maybe I'd found a kindred spirit, someone else who understood The Flow was all there was, and that all the rest was imaginative human invention. The constant giveaway that I hadn't met such a soul mate was these mavericks' sense of bravado. They treated the by-laws like dragons to be slain. To set out to slay a dragon, says my logic, you have to believe a dragon exists. What's more, slaying any kind of enemy needs a violent frame of mind, and it turned out that all the mavericks I met were prone to violence. Not one had the vision to see that there were no dragons to slay, and that without an enemy, weapons and violence were lunacy.

When I began my travels, I found it the same everywhere I went. The games, and the rules of the games, were different, to be sure, even though the by-laws of different Associations' turned out to be surprisingly alike—as did the maverick violence. The by-laws were always enshrined up there on an airy pedestal. There were always fights over what the by-laws actually intended. There were always some people who wanted to write new by-laws altogether—so long as they were the ones who got to write them. I long ago accepted the human desire, compulsion, even, to invent games that can make life more varied, or interesting, entertaining or challenging, games that can even give human life here a simulated logic and order it doesn't seem to have.

In fact, I did more than just accept this human need; I delighted in it. There was such a wealth and variety of imagery, color, sounds and music, smells and tastes, touching and kissing and dancing that went with it all, celebrations of all the senses that made humans human. The stories that went with these rituals evoked laughter and tears, fear, mystery, wonder and awe—all the feelings that made humans human. My delight, though, was tempered with sadness from the start. What was so close to being a species' celebration of itself always took a sour turn. It was so clear to me that the curvature of the human skull was bending things askew. The players were so caught up in the games of their own making that they were prepared to kill to win—or die in the attempt. It was all so clear to me, from my vantage point of The Flow, but that view stayed hidden from the rest.

I've always been on the sidelines, watching, there, in the stands, all by myself. When I was young, I felt like shouting, "Hey, you guys, remember it's only a game! It doesn't matter!" I knew, alas, that however loudly I shouted, my voice could never be heard above the clamor of the playing field. And what use, anyway, asking the players to "remember" something they'd never known and so, couldn't have forgotten? I wanted to call a time out when darkness fell, to urge the players to look at the moon and the stars to remind themselves of what and where they, the players, were. But I knew that wouldn't have been any use, either; the floodlights in the stadium were so bright the players wouldn't have been able to see the night sky.

Did I come to feel lonely and depressed? It may surprise you when I tell you that I felt quite the opposite. I felt an elation, a heady sense of power. I could choose any game I wanted to play, yes, but I could do something more than that: I could invent my own game with no rules and no by-laws other than the ones I chose to play by. I, and I alone, knew that nothing said I had to be kind to anyone. I could make someone cry if I wanted to. Or make them smile. I knew I didn't have to be honest or tell the truth, though I could if I wanted to. I knew that nothing I might do was either right or wrong. As for my being a part of some looming Armageddon between the forces of Good and Evil, well, that game appealed to many, but not to me, and nothing said I had to play any game I didn't like.

Imagine! Here it is, a tiny speck of stuff spinning through the infinite, an accidental conglomeration of vibrations, just doing its thing for a while. Suddenly I turn up, and in a form that can give this random bit of fluff meaning—meaning of which it has none without me. And I can give it any meaning I want. Wow! That's heady stuff.

But it's your birthright, too. While you're here as a sentient, individual human being, you can take anything your senses bring to you and give it whatever meaning you want. *Anything*—from the Himalayas to that tiniest of weeds pushing its way up through the concrete slabs of a city street; from the grandest of symphonies to the first, anguished wail of a newborn; from the scent of a freshly cut lemon to the reek of burnt flesh; from the sweetness of milk and honey to the disgust of vomit in the throat; from the searing laceration of a whip to the comfort of a caress. It's all yours, and yours to make whatever you want of. You can choose to put all of your experience into someone else's structure that appeals to you, to mix and match from the many, many structures people have invented, or you can come up with a totally new structure of your own. Whatever you do, the ongoing event "out there" will go on as it always has and always will.

If I could leave you that knowledge of your individual omnipotence, as I'd so very much like to, you wouldn't have to look for omnipotence in other places anymore. I'd be giving you the ability to enjoy, fully, the richness of the human experience. You'd feel able to revel in one another's various constructions and rituals—with no sense of rivalry or domination. You'd feel eager to share with one another the things you've found that bring you joy—with no sense of ownership or exclusivity. You'd feel free to try out all human experiences and all human feelings—with no sense of either judgment or guilt.

That knowledge would be for you as great a gift as it has been for me. I came among you already knowing that no moment of mine, no act of mine, no emotion of mine, meant anything at all against the backdrop in front of which I would briefly pass. Knowing that has let me give each of my moments, each of my acts, each of my emotions, the most intense of meanings in the here and now.

For me, that here and now is almost over. These days, I look to the sun and the shadows around me that mark the turning of the Earth with an increasing feeling of security. As evening comes, I lie in my hammock by the pond and look to the moon and the stars with certainty and trust. I feel an approaching expansion in my being. I feel my skin getting too tight to hold what's been bound up in it for this little while. What's been confined in human form is about to be part of that wonderment again, part of the whirl and dance that ever changes even as it stays the same. I feel an accelerating exhilaration. I, as in the "me" that people know, won't be here anymore, and there'll be no "me" to be anywhere else—except everywhere at once and forever.

But while there is still a "me" in this skin to go on wrestling with words, I'll think of you as I leave you this message, scratching my old head over how on earth to give you possession of the freedom that is yours. I'll think of you—yes, even *you*, O nameless, faceless shadow who assaulted me that night in Pernambuco—with great fondness. I almost said with love, but writing all these words has made me too skittish about using them to end this song on that particular note. The only thing I know for sure about love is that whatever it means to you exists nowhere else in all The Flow but here. It exists only in the human mind. It has no significance beyond the human skull. Whether that makes love something of no consequence or, on the other hand, makes it a treasure beyond price, is up to you to decide—as is what you decide to do about love while you're here.

The news was indeed blood-red again tonight. More temples of the human spirit blown to shreds in the name of chimeras of your own invention. And thus it will continue unless and until . . . unless and until . . . unless and until *what?* Unless and until you can come to value and embrace those mindless, whirling galaxies "out there" because their indifference gives you value and meaning.

> Farewell all joys, O Death, come close mine eyes.
> More geese than swans now live, more fools than wise.

That's how the song ends, and I'm ready for bed. If tonight's the night for death to come close mine eyes, so be it. The world will be no poorer for one less goose. But, oh, my beloved ugly ducklings, if only you could see yourselves for the swans you could become!